POISON PEN

Raven Hill Mysteries 10

Emily Rodda & Mary Forrest

Hodder
Children's
Books

a division of Hodder Headline plc

Series concept copyright © Emily Rodda 1994
Text copyright © Ashton Scholastic 1994

First published in Australia in 1994 by
Ashton Scholastic Pty Limited

First published in Great Britain in 1998
by Hodder Children's Books

A Catalogue record for this book is
available from the British Library

ISBN 0 340 71481 6

Printed and bound in Great Britain by
Mackays of Chatham PLC, Chatham, Kent

Hodder Children's Books
A Division of Hodder Headline plc
338 Euston Road
London NW1 3BH

Contents

1

Mysteries

'Elmo Zimmer, would you *please* stop that talking and get on with your work! Unless you feel you have nothing to learn from this class. In which case you can get out!'

I jumped, and turned back to the front. Ms Adair, our English teacher, my favourite teacher, was glaring at me. I felt myself starting to blush.

The class had gone very quiet. For a start, they weren't used to hearing me get ticked off. Unlike, say, Tom Moysten, who's always joking and playing the fool and getting into trouble, I keep a pretty low profile at school.

But Ms Adair hardly ever shouted at anyone, anyway. And she usually didn't mind us talking if we kept the noise level down. She thought it helped us get our ideas straight if we discussed things.

But not today, it seemed. Today she stood there with her mouth set in a straight line and her black eyebrows drawn together, just waiting for anyone else to get out of line.

So no-one did. Not even Tom. He might have played up on another teacher. Some of the teachers at Raven Hill High are so crabby that he seems to feel it's his duty to keep them at boiling point. But Ms Adair isn't like that—not usually, anyway.

'Phew—I'm glad that's over. What's wrong with Adair, do you reckon?' Nick Kontellis asked, as the Teen Power gang finally escaped at the end of the lesson and headed for the gate.

We had a job interview that afternoon. Nothing very interesting—just casual cleaning for a woman called Mrs Drisk-Haskell—but money's money, as Nick always says. Our job agency's called Teen Power Inc. and we say we'll do anything. We will too—as long as it's part-time, and legal.

'Something's worrying her.' Liz Free hurried along beside us, still doing up her backpack, and clutching a million other bits and pieces in her hands as usual. 'She looks really tired, don't you think? As if she's not sleeping. That can really affect people. Poor thing.'

Richelle Brinkley, the glamour girl of our group, shook back her long, blonde hair. 'That's no excuse!' she sniffed. 'I mean, I've got personal problems myself at the moment. And *I'm* not screaming at people.'

'The fact that you might, stress *might*, need to get glasses for reading hardly qualifies as a major tragedy, Richelle,' Sunny Chan said flatly.

'No, Richelle,' Liz put in. 'I don't know why you're carrying on. There's nothing wrong with glasses. Millions of people wear glasses. Ms Adair for one.'

'Oh, you're so comforting!' exclaimed Richelle sarcastically. 'You mean that if I'm *really* lucky I can get to look just like Ms Adair! Thanks a lot. I'll do my best. I'll just have to gain a bit of weight and get wrinkles round my eyes and a bad haircut and—'

We turned out of the school gate and headed up the road.

'Elmo wears reading glasses,' Tom pointed out. 'He seems to bear up okay.'

Richelle sniffed again. Obviously she thought that nothing that happened to the way I looked would be a problem to me. Short guys with curly red hair and freckles and boring clothes aren't Richelle's idea of fashion leaders. I wonder why?

'Anyway, whatever's wrong with Adair she's got no business taking it out on everyone else,' Nick said. 'It's stupid to get yourself into such a state that you can't sleep or do your job properly. It's just unprofessional.'

'Oh, what would you know about it, Nick?' Liz burst out passionately. 'You're so superior, aren't you? You might feel differently if something awful happened to you!'

Nick raised an eyebrow and looked down his nose at her. But Sunny, Tom and I glanced at each other. We knew why Liz was so upset. The bank where her mother works had been held up the week before. The guys had

had guns, and one of the other tellers had been killed.

Liz had told us that her mother was still having nightmares about it. She was really stressed out, Liz said, and was finding it hard to work. Especially since the cops seemed to have decided the robbers must have had inside information about the bank, and kept interviewing the staff over and over again.

'Listen, Elmo,' Tom said brightly, obviously wanting to break up the tension. 'I've got a great idea. Why don't you ask The Eye to spy on Ms Adair and find out what's wrong with her? If The Eye can't do it, who can?'

He was talking about this new column in my dad's newspaper, the *Pen*. It was a sort of gossip column, with lots of bits and pieces in it about doings in Raven Hill. Little, funny things that most people didn't know. The column was always just signed 'The Eye'.

Sunny laughed, and even Liz gave a sort of smile, so I played along. 'You're right. The Eye's the answer,' I said. 'Or would be, Tom, if anyone had the faintest idea who The Eye was!'

'Is that really true? *Really*, Elmo?' asked Liz curiously. 'Surely Zim knows who writes the column. He must.'

I shook my head. 'Dad doesn't have any idea,' I said. 'Cross my heart.'

'Go on. He writes it himself!' Nick scoffed. 'Bet you a million bucks.'

'You lose,' I told him. 'If Dad wrote it I'd know. The column turns up at the office every week in a brown envelope addressed to him, just like it did the first time.

4

It's signed "The Eye", it comes through the ordinary mail, just postmarked Raven Hill. There's no way of telling who sent it.'

'What about the payment, Zimmer?' drawled Nick. He thought he'd caught me out on that one.

'We don't pay for it,' I told him. 'How can we? We wouldn't know who to pay. Dad just reads the copy to make sure there's nothing wrong with it, then prints it. End of story.'

'You don't *pay* for it?' Nick murmured, his dark eyes thoughtful. 'That's weird. Everyone turns to the Eye column first now, after only a month. The Eye could make a lot of money out of it. Zim'd pay well. He must know it's the best thing in the paper.'

I didn't say anything. Nick has this way of running down the *Pen* whenever he gets the chance. It makes me really mad. The Eye adds something to the paper. Of course it does. But there are a lot of other good things in the *Pen* as well.

'Listen, this is really *great*,' exclaimed Liz, looking quite excited. She loves a mystery. 'An anonymous watcher, keeping an eye on Raven Hill. Who on earth could it be?'

Sunny shrugged. 'Could be anyone.'

'Not anyone,' Nick argued. He was getting curious now, too. I could tell. 'The bits of info in the column are a huge mix. Everything from fights in the flower club to fires in the fire-station and runaway goats in the mall. The Eye is someone who knows a lot of things that other people don't.'

'Well, I don't think The Eye's so special,' Richelle put in, opening her big blue eyes wide. 'Like, *we'd* heard about the big fight at the flower-arranging club before it was in the column. My mother told me about it, and I told you. It was *awful*, Mum said. She said—'

'Dear, oh dear,' sighed Tom, shaking his head. 'Violence among the violets. Fighting in the ferns. Looniness among the lilies. Murder in the marigolds. Scandal in the . . . um . . .'

'Snapdragons,' Sunny suggested helpfully. 'And *I'd* heard about the white cockatoo eating that woman's window-frames, for example. I heard about it at the gym a couple of weeks ago.'

By now we were walking down one of the crescents on the far side of Raven Hill Road, where all the big old houses are. Liz stopped and fished around in her pocket until she found a grubby scrap of paper.

'The point is,' she said impatiently, looking up and around, 'because of school and our Teen Power jobs, most of us might have already heard one or two of the Eye stories every week. For that matter, I suppose a lot of people have. But The Eye puts them all together. It's fascinating! And such a mystery! Listen, guys, we cross here. There's the Drisk-Haskell house, over there. The big white one.'

We stared for a moment at the huge mansion in front of us. Then Tom bent over and hunched up one shoulder. He began pretending to drool, and tugged at the front of his hair.

'Your humble cleaners be here, Mrs Drisk-Haskell,' he slurred, shuffling forward. 'Arr. Will ye be wantin' us to muck out the stables, first, m'lady, or clean the lavs?'

Richelle looked disgusted, and Sunny and Liz started to giggle. And so Liz's fascinating Eye mystery was forgotten.

But not for long.

2

Mrs Drisk-Haskell

Just inside the vast iron gates, Richelle stopped and wrinkled her nose. 'We're supposed to clean *this* place?' she complained, looking down the long, red-gravelled drive to the house. 'It's *huge*.'

'We're only filling in for a week or so. Only till Mrs Drisk-Haskell can find a regular cleaner,' Liz said hastily.

'Then why does she need to interview us?' Nick demanded.

Liz shrugged. 'She's particular about who she has working for her. The Matron at "Craigend" recommended us. I spoke to her when I went to visit Miss Plummer on Friday, and she said that Mrs Drisk-Haskell pays well, but she's also *very* fussy. So nobody do anything awful. Okay?'

'Arr,' gurgled Tom, nodding violently and wiping his nose on his sleeve. Liz poked him sharply in the ribs and we set off up the long winding drive.

Mrs Drisk-Haskell turned out to be an elegant

middle-aged woman with ultra-blonde hair that had
been hairsprayed into the shape of a helmet. She was
wearing a beige suit that didn't look particularly special
to me. But I could see Richelle gazing at it in
admiration, so I guessed that it must be a designer
model.

'How nice of you to come,' she gushed as she led us
into her huge, sunny lounge room. 'I do admire you for
taking on all these jobs. It's wonderful to come across
some young people who aren't afraid of hard work.'

Liz murmured something polite and Mrs Drisk-
Haskell beamed at her. She stroked the rope of pearls
about her neck and went on chatting.

'Mind you, I *never* had to work myself, when I was a
young thing. I've always been spoilt, first by my parents
and then by my late husband. He was a wonderful man.
You may have heard of him—Reginald Drisk-Haskell?'

We all looked blank. Her voice sharpened. 'The
Drisk-Haskells are a *very* old, established Raven Hill
family,' she told us, as if wondering whether people as
ignorant as we were would be suitable cleaners for her
after all.

I stared at her in fascination. The others seemed to
have other interests. Liz and Sunny were concentrating
on keeping Tom in line. Nick was gazing at the antique
furniture, probably trying to work out its value. Richelle
was looking around furtively to see how much cleaning
we were in for.

'I've been told all about you,' Mrs Drisk-Haskell

continued, frowning slightly. 'I must say, I was most impressed by your backgrounds.'

She ran her eyes across us and focused on Sunny. 'You must be the doctor's little girl,' she said. She touched the back of her hair-helmet. 'I don't actually go to your mother, dear—Reg always *insisted* on sending me to a specialist in the city—but I've heard that she does marvellous work. And which one of you is the *Pen* editor's son? Elmo Zimmer the third?'

I shuffled my feet. 'Um—I am,' I heard myself mumbling.

Mrs Drisk-Haskell turned towards me and her smile froze. I got the impression that she would have liked to put a few sheets of newspaper across my chair before I sat down. I couldn't see why. My clothes might be old, but they're reasonably clean.

'Fancy that,' she said faintly. 'I'm sure you must be very proud of your father. Reg knew your grandfather, of course, because they were both involved in doing charity work around Raven Hill. He always said that your grandfather was a true gentleman—such charming manners and so well dressed.'

She gave me a long hard look, as if she hoped that I'd get the message and start wearing snazzy three-piece suits and a full beard, like Grandad. Then she moved on to tell Liz that Reg once almost bought a house from Free and Somers, the real estate firm where Liz's dad is a partner.

She also told Richelle that Reg would have thought

she was a real little beauty. And she told Tom that she was pleased to hear his father was a teacher, because Reg always said that teachers were the backbone of society.

'Brian's not my father,' Tom muttered. 'He's my stepfather. My father's a painter.'

Mrs Drisk-Haskell's eyebrows shot up and she gave Tom another of her long hard looks. She was obviously disappointed in him, just like she'd been disappointed in me.

'Well,' she said briskly, after a moment. 'I suppose we'd better get down to business now.'

I couldn't help noticing that she hadn't said anything to Nick at all. It looked as though the famous Reg hadn't approved of the Greek families in Raven Hill, however successful and rich they were. I glanced secretly across at Nick, wondering whether he minded. But he was just studying Mrs Drisk-Haskell with his usual superior smile.

'That's a good idea,' he drawled. 'How often do you want us to come?'

'Twice a week, I think,' she replied. 'My old cleaner came once a week, but she spent the whole day. And she brought her daughter with her as well, so perhaps you had better work in pairs. Why don't I show you around, to give you an idea of the size of the house?'

As she led us from one room to the next, she kept pointing out the expensive vases and the antique furniture and the paintings by well-known artists.

'Reg bought so many beautiful things for this house,'

she sighed. 'It's such a responsibility. I'll give you my phone number before you leave, but it's unlisted and you'll have to promise me that you won't pass it on to anyone else. Still, I'm sure I can trust you lovely young people. Matron said you'd be a perfect stop-gap for me, until I can find a permanent cleaner. And Reg always trusted Matron's judgment.'

By now I was sick of hearing about wonderful Reg and I was definitely starting to dislike Mrs Drisk-Haskell. She was snobbish and super-confident and incredibly annoying.

So I was pleased when Richelle smiled sweetly and said, 'Mrs Drisk-Haskell, if you're looking for a regular cleaner, why don't you try this lady called Mrs Flower? She works for us and my mother says she's wonderful. I could give you her number.'

Richelle doesn't like cleaning jobs—and she doesn't like being patronised either. She obviously thought that suggesting Mrs Flower would be a good way to get out of cleaning Mrs Drisk-Haskell's enormous house. But for some reason Mrs Drisk-Haskell looked straight through her and pretended that she hadn't heard.

I decided to give Richelle a bit of help.

'Hey, that's a good idea,' I said enthusiastically. 'Mrs Flower has just started cleaning the *Pen* office in the early mornings, too. My father's crazy about her. He reckons she's the most reliable cleaner we've ever had.'

Richelle nodded eagerly and we stared at Mrs Drisk-Haskell in unison, trying to force her to answer. For once she actually looked slightly confused and taken aback. She clutched at her rope of pearls and cleared her throat several times.

Then she said, 'That's very kind of you. But as a matter of fact, Mrs Flower was my old cleaner. She worked here for many years. But, unfortunately, I had to—ah—let her go.'

3

The mastermind at work

As soon as we got out of Mrs Drisk-Haskell's house, and were safely out of earshot, we all started to talk at once. Tom has the loudest voice, so he managed to shout the rest of us down.

'I hate the fancy way that woman talks,' he exploded. 'She had to "let Mrs Flower go". What a ridiculous thing to say. Why can't she just admit that she sacked her?'

'I wonder what Mrs Flower did?' Sunny said thoughtfully. 'Do you reckon she broke things, or forgot to dust the paintings, or what?'

I snorted. 'She probably wasn't sacked at all. She probably just decided she couldn't stand Mrs Drisk-Haskell any more, and left. Mrs Flower's a pretty tough customer. I'm surprised that she managed to work here for five minutes without telling Mrs Drisk-Haskell what she thought of her. Let alone for years.'

'That sounds right,' Nick agreed. 'Drisk-Haskell would drive most people crazy. She's really up herself.'

His voice sounded unexpectedly bitter and I started to wonder whether he had cared about the way Mrs Drisk-Haskell ignored him, after all. He stared back at me with expressionless eyes.

'All right, what are we going to do now?' he asked. 'Elmo, how about dropping in at the *Pen* to take a look at an original manuscript of one of The Eye's columns? Would that be possible?'

So he hadn't forgotten the mystery. Trust Nick.

'Sure,' I said. 'And you don't even have to look at old ones. It's Monday, so the new column should have arrived in today's mail. You can get a preview.'

Sunny had to go to a gym class, but the others decided to come along to the *Pen* with Nick and me. While we all strolled back to the main road, Tom did some imitations of Mrs Drisk-Haskell that had the rest of us laughing until we were out of breath—even Nick.

'That's better,' Sunny gasped finally. 'I feel as though I've laughed her out of my system now.'

As we crossed Raven Hill Road, Liz remembered that she had to buy some bones for her dog, Christo. We detoured down to the butcher's shop in the Mall, but Richelle refused to go inside.

'I can't stand Sam Frean,' she announced. 'He calls me "girlie".'

'He could call you worse things,' said Tom darkly.

'Like . . .'

Richelle ignored him. 'Plus he keeps asking whether I've got a boyfriend. And he always reminds me of the time when I opened one of Mum's parcels and started eating raw mince. I was only two years old at the time. You'd think he'd have forgotten about it by now. But oh, no.'

'He sounds wonderful,' Tom said cheerfully. 'Like my kind of guy. Cheerful. I can't wait to meet him.'

But as we crowded into the shop, the butcher looked up at us with a face like thunder. He served Liz with an unsmiling face and barely answered when she tried to chat to him.

'What's the matter, Sam?' she asked sympathetically. 'Aren't you feeling well?'

'Of course I am,' he snapped. 'Why shouldn't I be? The shop's been very quiet today, that's all. I've got out of the habit of talking.'

He turned away and began to heap a huge pile of bones onto the scales.

'Hey!' Tom teased. 'Hey, Liz. You don't want Christo to starve. Are you sure Sam's giving you enough?'

He waited for the butcher to laugh, but instead Sam Frean swung around and marched back to the counter.

'What do you mean by that?' he demanded belligerently. 'Don't you trust me? Here, check the scales for yourself. The young lady asked for three kilos of bones and that's what she's getting. A bit more, if anything.'

16

Tom tried to explain that he'd just been joking, but the butcher stood over him until he read out the figures on the scales. Liz handed over the money with a shaking hand and we escaped from the shop.

Richelle strolled up to us. 'How was Sam the joker?' she murmured. 'He didn't seem to be carrying on as much as he usually does. He must have been on his best behaviour. You were lucky.'

'No, we weren't,' Liz said angrily. 'He was absolutely horrible to us. Tom made a perfectly ordinary joke and Sam went wild as though he was being accused of being dishonest. He made Tom check the scales.'

'How *embarrassing*,' Richelle said with a shudder. 'I'm glad I didn't go in with you.'

Tom scowled at her and Sunny hastily reminded us that we were supposed to be heading for the *Pen* office.

'I wish I could come too,' she said wistfully, 'but I have to go to gym. Don't forget to tell me everything that you can find out about The Eye.'

When we arrived at the *Pen*, we went straight out to the big back room where the journalists and subeditors worked. Dad came bustling out from his office to meet us, flourishing a page of print.

'Look, Elmo!' he exclaimed. 'The latest Eye column. It arrived this morning and I had it keyed-in this afternoon. You have to read it—this one's even funnier than last week's.'

He put the page out on his desk and we leaned over it, chuckling from time to time and pointing out our favourite bits.

After we'd finished, Nick turned to Dad and said politely, 'Listen, Zim, would you mind showing us the original copy? And would you still have the envelope it came in?'

'You've decided to track down The Eye, have you?' Dad's tired eyes twinkled at him. 'Well, I wish you luck. Elmo and I have done our best, and failed miserably.'

I dug in the recycling bin and found the envelope. 'See how you go on this,' I said, handing it over to Nick.

Nick held the envelope up to the light and studied it intently.

'Plain brown envelope,' he said. 'The cheap sort sold in packets all over the place. The address has obviously been cut out of the *Pen*.'

'Yeah. It's part of the notice that runs on the front page every week, calling for letters and things,' I told him.

Nick nodded impatiently. He didn't want my help. 'Raven Hill postmark,' he went on slowly. 'That suggests that The Eye lives or works in Raven Hill.'

'Well, of course!' exclaimed Liz. 'The column's all about local gossip. Only someone who spends a lot of time here could do it.'

'Don't interrupt the mastermind, Liz,' murmured Tom. 'The great brain needs perfect peace and quiet to operate.'

'Were the other envelopes like this too, Zim?' Nick asked, ignoring them.

Dad nodded. 'Down to the last detail.' He handed over two sheets of paper. 'Here's the original manuscript, Nick. Go for it.' He folded his arms and watched, smiling.

Nick opened the envelope and pulled out two sheets of paper. 'Written on a computer,' he said, sounding disappointed. 'Nothing unusual about it.'

'I told you,' I said smugly. 'And look at this.' I pointed to the heading at the top of the first page.

'"Written exclusively for the Raven Hill *Pen*,"' Nick read aloud. '"May be used free of charge." How weird.'

Richelle had been staring off into space as usual, twiddling her hair. Suddenly she focused on Nick. 'So have you found any clues yet?' she yawned.

'It's not that easy,' he grumbled. 'There'd be no point in testing for fingerprints. The envelope's been handled by too many people. Still, the cops could probably work out The Eye's blood type by analysing the spit on the envelope. Why don't you hand it over to them, Zim?'

'Because I don't want to waste their time,' Zim said dryly. 'I know we're all very curious about The Eye, Nick, but I don't think the police would be particularly interested in unmasking an anonymous newspaper columnist—especially not when they've got a bank robbery and a murder to investigate. Besides, it's all right with me if The Eye wants to hide behind a pen-name. The column's done wonders for the paper. It's just what we need.'

Stephen Spiers, the *Pen*'s senior reporter, butted in at this point. He'd been listening to Nick and Dad from the next desk.

'Personally, I think The Eye's overrated,' he sniffed. 'There's no hard news in the column, just local trivia. Half of it's old stuff, anyway. I told you ten days ago about Tony's deli and the dog that stole the salami. And everyone knows about the shepherd's-pie strike at the hospital.'

'Not everyone,' Zim said with a grin. 'And it's the way it's told that counts. The column's funny, Steve. It's light-hearted. People love it. And I'll tell you something else—it's living history too.'

'What do you mean?' Stephen Spiers asked with a puzzled frown.

'Well, not many people remember this, but there was a *Pen* column signed "The Eye" back in my father's time. I suspect that Molly Beer, one of the journalists, used to write it, though Dad would never let on. At any rate, the column stopped when she died and it never started up again. Not until now.'

Dad nodded thoughtfully, lost in his memories. His eyes were shining and he was smiling to himself.

'She was a real character, old Molly, and an excellent writer as well,' he said softly. 'I think she'd be proud of the new Eye. It looks simple, Steve, but it isn't.

It takes talent to put a column like this together. Talent, a love of people, and a good observing eye.'

I grinned affectionately at him, feeling a warm glow inside me. Dad had worked hard to pull the *Pen* together again after Grandad died, and it was great to see him looking so happy. He was right too. The Eye was exactly what the *Pen* needed.

No matter what Stephen Spiers said.

4

Eyes right

The next day at school there was big news. Ms Adair had resigned.

Liz was really upset, and so was I.

'I told you something was wrong,' Liz wailed at lunchtime. 'I *told* you. Oh, maybe she's got some terrible illness, or something. Why else would she go?'

'There are a million other reasons,' Nick muttered. 'She might have just got sick of teaching. Wouldn't you? Imagine facing Moysten over a poetry book every day of your life.'

He tried to get his usual jeering act into full swing, but his heart wasn't in it. I think everyone was sorry to lose a good teacher like Ms Adair. All the rotten teachers seemed set to stay in Raven Hill High for life.

We went off to our English class that afternoon determined to ask Ms Adair to change her mind. At least, Liz, Sunny, Tom and I were determined. Nick and Richelle told us it would be pointless, and we'd just embarrass ourselves. But we wanted to try anyway. We talked to a lot of the other kids, and they agreed. No-one wanted Ms Adair to go.

So the minute Ms Adair walked into the room, Liz rose to her feet.

'Ms Adair,' she began, 'on behalf of the whole class I want to—'

Then she stopped in mid-sentence, because Ms Adair wasn't listening. Instead, she was staring angrily at two kids in the front row. They had a copy of the *Pen* open on the desk, and they were giggling together over the Eye column. Ms Adair's face went scarlet.

'I don't believe it,' she yelled at the top of her voice. 'How *could* you bring that rubbish into my class? This is the last straw!' She swung around and stormed out of the room.

There was a long moment of shocked silence and then the kids with the *Pen* swivelled around to face the rest of us.

'What did we do wrong?' one of them asked in confusion. 'I'm using the *Pen* for my media essay. I didn't know that Ms Adair was so dead set against it.'

'She's not,' Liz said. 'Or she never has been before. I don't think the *Pen*'s the problem at all, Robbie. It couldn't be. She's upset about something else, and she just, sort of, flew off the handle for no reason.'

'It doesn't make sense,' frowned Tom.

I sat still, with a nasty feeling gnawing at the pit of my stomach. Tom was right. It didn't make sense. And

23

I'd seen Ms Adair's face when she caught sight of the *Pen*. From where I was sitting, the expression in her eyes had seemed very close to hatred.

○

After school the Teen Power gang met up briefly outside the gates. Nick announced that he wanted us to go back to the *Pen* office, so that he could investigate The Eye a bit more.

'Not now,' Liz said, looking hassled. 'I'm going home for a while. I promised Dad. Mum was interviewed by the police again yesterday, and she's all upset.'

'They don't think *she* helped the bank robbers, do they?' asked Richelle nervously.

'Of course not!' Liz snapped. 'As if!'

'Well, they've spoken to her three times,' Richelle pointed out. 'They must have a reason.'

'Get your foot out of your mouth, will you, Richelle?' drawled Nick.

Liz flushed and turned away.

'Tom and I have to go and clean for the lovely Mrs Drisk-Haskell, Nick,' Sunny said, quickly changing the subject. 'But we could meet you at the *Pen* afterwards, if you like.'

'What about you, Elmo?' Nick asked hopefully, but I shook my head.

'Sorry, I've got to see the optometrist this

afternoon. I have a regular six-monthly check up and I can't miss it.'

Richelle gave a strangled squeak and we all turned to look at her.

'What's the matter?' I asked. As if I didn't know.

She sighed deeply.

'It's that word—optometrist,' she whispered with a shudder.

'Richelle!' snorted Liz in exasperation. 'Really, you—'

'You don't understand, Liz,' Richelle wailed pathetically. 'It's actually happened! My mother actually made the appointment. I have to go on Thursday. To this Mr Salamandi person, in Craigend Road. Oh, he's going to make me wear glasses, I know he is! I'll have to wear glasses, and they'll make me look absolutely hideous.'

'Ms Salamandi's a she, not a he,' I said. 'I go to her as well. She's okay. She'll look after you.'

Richelle hunched her shoulders like some poor bedraggled bird. She was really taking all this glasses business to heart. Even though I knew she was being ridiculous, I felt quite sorry for her.

'Listen, why don't you come along with me today?' I suggested on impulse. 'You could check out some of the glasses frames Ms Salamandi's got on show. See what's available.'

I didn't expect Richelle to take me seriously. I'd only made the offer because she was looking so crushed and miserable. But to my surprise she brightened up straightaway.

'Could I really go with you?' she asked eagerly. 'That'd be great. Part of my problem is that I just can't *stand* the strain of waiting. I just can't help it. I'm very sensitive and—'

'Yeah, we all know how sensitive you are, Richelle,' Nick interrupted with a grin. 'Like a little flower, aren't you? Why don't I come along and hold your hand while you try on the frames? Then we can all meet at the *Pen* later on.'

I groaned quietly to myself. That would teach me to feel sorry for Richelle Brinkley. Now I was stuck with her—and to make things even worse, I was stuck with super-cool Nick as well.

It was quite an experience, walking through Raven Hill with Nick and Richelle. They swanned down Craigend Road like royalty, talking together in loud confident voices. Both of them were so tall and good-looking that I started to feel like their grubby younger brother. To use Richelle's favourite word, it was embarrassing.

By the time we arrived at the optometrist's, I was ready to pretend that I'd never seen Richelle before in my life. However, she didn't need any more help from me. Richelle still regularly gets lost on her way to class, but she can find her way around shops and malls and department stores by instinct, like a homing pigeon. She walked into Ms Salamandi's reception area, strode past the receptionist's desk and went straight on into the little room where the glasses frames were on display.

The receptionist looked up with a start. 'Who was that?' she said, making a feeble attempt to snap at me.

I understood how she felt. Richelle had looked straight through her. She's not the sort of person Richelle notices. She's not old and she's not young. She's not plain, but she's not good-looking. And she wears grey skirts and beige blouses and grey cardigans. The sort of clothes Richelle wouldn't look at twice. Or even once.

'I'm sorry, Miss—um, I'm sorry,' I mumbled, realising too late that I didn't know her name, even though I'd been coming to the optometrist for years. I was as bad as Richelle. Almost.

'Do you know that girl?' the receptionist demanded, looking as though she would have liked a good excuse to throw Richelle out.

'Sort of,' I stammered. 'I mean—yes, I do. Her name's Richelle Brinkley and she's coming in for an appointment on Thursday and she just wanted to—'

The receptionist sighed heavily. 'Oh, I see. All right.' She turned back to her typing with a twitch of her shoulder that said, 'don't bother explaining, I just work here, that's all.'

Meanwhile, Nick was inspecting the waiting room with a disdainful stare. There was nothing much to look at—just some dark wood panelling and a few rickety chairs and a stack of very old magazines.

The man in the far corner must have known about the magazines. He'd brought his own copy of the *Pen* with him and he was reading it through mega-thick glasses with heavy black frames. I hoped that Richelle wouldn't spot him. If she thought she was going to end up with glasses like that, she'd really freak out.

Luckily for me, she hurtled out of the display room so fast that she didn't notice anyone. 'Get me out of here,' she hissed, clutching Nick's sleeve. 'I can't stay in this place another minute. It's too *depressing*.'

The receptionist looked daggers at her, but Nick grinned and patted her arm.

'We'll go and get something to eat,' he told me. 'Why don't you meet us in the Black Cat after your appointment? You'll be going straight back to the *Pen*, won't you?'

The man in the corner lowered his newspaper and stared at me curiously. I was sure he was about to say something, but at that moment Richelle and Nick sauntered between us, blocking his view.

Then a young man with watery eyes blundered out of Ms Salamandi's office, blinking furiously, and the receptionist glanced across and said, 'All right, Mr Richardson, you can go in now.'

'Thank you, dear,' he said with a patronising smile. He carefully folded his newspaper, put it into his briefcase, and took himself into the office.

Mr Richardson, I thought to myself. The name

seemed vaguely familiar, but I was sure I hadn't seen him before.

So why did he look as though he was really keen to speak to me?

5

Quick changes

A few seconds later Ms Salamandi came beetling out of
her office. She's a small, energetic and rather brusque
woman who doesn't believe in wasting time.

'You've given me the wrong card again,' she
snapped at the receptionist. 'I need Mr Richardson's
card, not Elmo's.'

The receptionist was still trying to take down the
watery-eyed young man's address. She lost her place in
the appointment book, dropped the cards and
scrabbled around on the floor, muttering to herself. Ms
Salamandi sighed impatiently. She pushed past her,
snatched up the right card and marched back into her
office.

I picked up an ancient *Reader's Digest* and started
leafing through it.

The receptionist thumped away at her typewriter.
Even from behind she looked depressed and
downtrodden.

So many people I meet seem to be miserable lately, I thought. Of course, Ms Salamandi's receptionist always *does* look miserable. But Ms Adair doesn't. She's usually really breezy and confident. And so, according to Liz, is Sam Frean the butcher. But both of them had changed. Really quickly, too. It was odd.

I was still puzzling about character changes when Ms Salamandi called me in. On first sight her office is rather alarming. There's a plastic model of an eye on her desk and posters of eyes all over the walls.

Still, I was used to the place by now. I settled down comfortably in the chair, while she flashed a series of cards in front of me, and peered into my eyes.

'That's good, Elmo,' she said after a few minutes. 'You won't need a new prescription this time. Off you go now. I'll see you again in six months time.'

When I came out into the waiting room, I noticed that the man called Mr Richardson was still hanging around, rearranging the papers in his briefcase. He fiddled with the papers until I'd finished organising my next appointment with the receptionist and then he snapped the case shut and walked out into the corridor with me.

'This is quite a coincidence,' he said in a hearty voice. 'I couldn't help overhearing what your friends said to you. So you work at the *Pen*, do you? Copy boy or something, are you?'

'Sort of,' I said vaguely. I didn't feel like explaining to some total stranger that my father was the editor of the *Pen*. For one thing, it was none of Mr Richardson's business. And for another, he was behaving a bit weirdly. I wanted to know more about him before I decided how much I was going to tell him.

While we headed down the stairs, he waffled on about how interesting it must be, working on a newspaper. Finally, just as we reached the doorway, he grabbed my arm.

'Tell me, would you like to make twenty dollars for yourself?' he asked in a low voice.

Uh-oh, I thought nervously, and pushed quickly past him into the street. Once we were on the footpath where there were plenty of other people around I turned to face him. 'What do you mean?' I asked loudly.

He winked at me.

'I want you to help me to settle a bet,' he murmured. 'Some of the chaps at the golf club were talking about this new column in the *Pen* the other day and we got very interested in the writer's identity. Can you tell me who The Eye is? As I said before, there's money in it for you.'

I felt rather relieved that that was all he wanted. But I was surprised, too. The Eye again. Suddenly everyone was on about The Eye. It was weird.

'Sorry,' I said. 'Nobody knows who The Eye is—not even the editor.'

Mr Richardson gave a jolly laugh. His thick glasses flashed in the sun. 'Come on, don't give me that,' he chuckled. 'Maybe the editor doesn't know but junior staff like you pick up on all the gossip. It's the same in my office as well. The staff know far more than the boss about what's going on around the place.'

I didn't say anything.

He leaned forward. 'Don't worry, son, this is just between you and me,' he muttered rapidly. 'I promise it won't go any further. You tell me, and no-one will ever know that you were the one who did. Is it a deal?'

He pulled a fat wallet out of the pocket of his suit and riffled through a wad of notes.

By now I'd decided that Mr Richardson was definitely a bit off. I backed away from him, shaking my head. He frowned, and then he shrugged, forcing a smile. He tore a page out of a notebook, and scribbled something on it.

'Oh well, you just think about it,' he said, handing me the paper. His fingers were damp with sweat, and shook slightly. 'If you change your mind, you can ring me at this number after six any night. Don't forget, I'll pay you twenty dollars—no, listen, make it fifty. Just keep our little talk to yourself, all right?'

He winked at me again and hurried off. I watched him go, frowning to myself. Fifty dollars, I thought. That's a lot of money. I wonder how much the bet was for.

Then I glanced at the scrap of paper and shook my head. Suddenly I felt sure that there was no bet. Mr Richardson had been incredibly nervous—much too nervous for a man who was only interested in settling a bet. He had some other reason for wanting to know about The Eye.

But what?

6

Mud sticks

I puzzled about Mr Richardson for a few minutes longer and then I put him out of my mind and went to collect Nick and Richelle from the Black Cat. We strolled along to the *Pen*, with Richelle raving on endlessly about her stupid glasses, while Nick concentrated on looking cool.

When we arrived at the office, I stopped in the doorway, so suddenly that Nick bumped into me.

'What's going on?' he asked, peering over my shoulder.

It was a pretty startling scene. Dad was bailed up in a corner with Mrs Flower menacing him, hands on hips. He looked startled and nervous. She looked furious. Mrs Flower's a big woman with tightly curled grey hair and those cat's-eye glasses that slant upwards and have rows of glittering stones at the edge of the frames. She's taller than Dad and much broader in the shoulders, and her mauve tracksuit didn't do anything to make her look

35

smaller or sweeter.

'I want some answers from you, Mr Zimmer,' she was shouting. 'From you and the *Pen*. You've got to tell me who The Eye is. And you'd better print something in your next issue, taking back everything The Eye said about me. If you won't, then I'll set the law onto you. I won't be slandered, Mr Zimmer. I know my rights. I've worked hard all my life and I—'

'Please, Mrs Flower, calm down,' Zim begged. 'I honestly don't know what you're talking about. There's been nothing in the Eye column about you. And I can't tell you who the columnist is, because I don't know.'

She snorted loudly. 'That's a laugh. It's your paper, isn't it? I don't believe you, Mr Zimmer. You're just trying to protect The Eye.'

My heart was beating at twice its usual speed. Impulsively I took a step forward and Richelle, who had been standing on tiptoe behind me trying to see, lost her footing and stumbled forward into the room.

Mrs Flower swung around and pointed at her dramatically. 'Ask Richelle Brinkley,' she exclaimed. 'Ask *her* if I haven't always been as honest as the day is long. She ought to know. I've worked for her mother for almost ten years.'

Richelle hates scenes. She turned bright scarlet and I could hear her whisper, 'How embarrassing.' But Mrs Flower kept pointing steadily at her until she muttered, 'Yes, of course.'

'There!' Mrs Flower said triumphantly. 'Richelle

agrees with me. So what's the *Pen* doing, dragging my reputation in the mud? That wicked Eye person is trying to ruin me. It's evil, that's what it is. Evil!'

Dad goggled at her, and rubbed his hand over his mouth. He obviously didn't know what to do.

I swallowed hard and clenched my fists tightly. None of this was making any sense to me.

'What—what has The Eye done to you, Mrs Flower?' I stammered finally.

'Done?' she repeated bitterly. 'The Eye's accused me of stealing. Me! As if I'd *ever* take *anything* that wasn't rightfully mine.'

I blinked at her in amazement. 'But like Dad said, there's been nothing in the column about you,' I protested. 'The Eye hasn't said a thing about you, Mrs Flower.'

'That's what you think,' she spat back. 'What about this? It came in the post today.'

She threw a note onto the desk. We all gathered around and stared at it. It was a message made up of words that had been cut from a newspaper and pasted onto a sheet of cheap notepaper:

IF PEOPLE KNEW ABOUT YOU THEY'D RUN YOU OUT OF RAVEN HILL. SOON I'LL SPREAD THE WORD. SERVES YOU RIGHT.

And it was signed with The Eye's by-line, cut out of the *Pen*.

'A poison-pen letter,' breathed Dad.

While Nick was hastily copying the words into his

notebook, Liz and Sunny and Tom came in. They took one look at the message and glanced at Mrs Flower, horrified.

'I told Mrs Drisk-Haskell that I never touched her stupid ring,' she roared. 'I said to her, "Mrs Drisk-Haskell," I said, "you've hidden it in some special place and forgotten where you put it. Or you've left it on a public washbasin or something. But no matter what's happened, it's got nothing to do with me."'

She looked around fiercely, as if daring us to disagree with her. Of course, none of us did. Dad nervously muttered something comforting.

'She didn't believe me,' Mrs Flower went on more quietly. 'Can you credit that? She told me to leave, just like that, after five years. Not that I would've stayed, anyway, after the things she'd said. She promised she wouldn't tell anyone, but now she's told this Eye person. And he's going to tell everyone.'

All of a sudden she burst into tears. Her glasses steamed up and her mauve shoulders heaved. Dad hovered around her, looking upset and helpless, and Liz rushed over to give her a box of tissues.

'If the word gets around, I've had it,' she sobbed. 'Who wants a light-fingered cleaner? Nobody with half a brain. The work will dry up and me and my daughter will be out on the street.'

'That's not true,' Liz said immediately. 'The people you work for know that you're reliable. They won't believe a whole lot of rumours.'

'No, but they'll believe The Eye,' Mrs Flower sniffled, taking off her glasses. She looked somehow more helpless without them. 'Everyone's been laughing over those columns in the *Pen* for weeks. If The Eye says it, then it's bound to be true. That's how most people will think, mark my words.'

Dad thrust his hands into his curly hair and tugged hard. 'This is terrible, Mrs Flower,' he said. 'I'll do something about it at once. I'm not quite sure what, but I'll definitely do something.'

Poor Mrs Flower gave a shuddering sigh, wiped her glasses and put them back on.

'Thanks, Mr Zimmer,' she said sadly. 'I'm sorry I shouted at you like that. My daughter's always telling me that I lose my temper first and ask questions afterwards, when it should be the other way around.'

'Don't worry about it,' Zim reassured her.

I was relieved that Mrs Flower was feeling friendly towards Dad again. But it was clear that whatever he'd said, she didn't think he had much chance of helping her. She said goodbye in a quiet, sad voice, quite unlike her usual one.

Once she had gone, we all looked at each other in dismay. Then everyone started talking at the same time, except for me. I felt so churned up that I couldn't even speak. It made me furious to think that anyone would want to get the *Pen* into so much trouble.

'Poor Mrs Flower,' Liz said. 'She's really worried and I can understand why. It must be dreadful to have someone telling lies about you like that.'

Richelle was looking thoughtful. 'There might be something in it, though, you know. The Eye doesn't usually get things wrong. I'd better tell Mum. She wouldn't want to have a thief for a cleaner.'

Tom and Sunny rounded on her together. 'Richelle Brinkley, you're *disgusting*,' Tom howled. 'How can you *say* such a thing, when there's absolutely no proof whatever that Mrs Flower took the ring? You're as bad as the Mrs Drisk-Haskell woman. And that means *really* bad.'

'Mrs Flower's been coming to your house for the past ten years, Richelle,' Sunny said more calmly. 'She's never stolen anything in that entire time. Why should she start now?'

'I don't know,' Richelle said with a shrug. 'But there could be all sorts of reasons. And we've got a lot of nice things in our house, you know, Sunny. You can't be too careful.'

Dad ran his hands through his hair again until it stuck out like steel wool. 'This is exactly what Mrs Flower was worried about,' he groaned. 'Mud sticks. Even if rumours are based on lies, some people will always go on suspecting that they might be true.'

He started to pace up and down the room, frowning to himself. 'I wonder whether I should withdraw The Eye's column from this week's edition, Elmo,' he murmured.

Nick flicked open his notebook. 'No, that won't

help Mrs Flower, Zim,' he said firmly. 'What we've got to do is work out who The Eye is, so we can put a stop to this.'

I shook my head violently at them both. 'You're just assuming The Eye wrote that poison-pen note, both of you,' I said. 'But why? Don't you see? It could be someone else entirely. Someone who used The Eye name so Mrs Flower would be scared, and blame the Pen. It could be that. Couldn't it?'

7

'It's crazy!'

Dad stopped pacing, and nodded. But Nick gave me one of his most superior smiles.

'Face facts, Elmo,' he said. 'I know you can't bear to believe that the *Pen* is associated with somebody who writes poison-pen letters. And I can see why you wouldn't want Zim to drop the most popular column that the *Pen*'s ever had. But—'

'There's no proof at all that The Eye's got anything to do with this,' I snapped angrily. 'The note to Mrs Flower wasn't typed on a computer, like the Eye columns are, for a start. It's crazy for you to assume The Eye wrote it.'

'Not totally crazy, Elmo,' Tom said unwillingly. 'Think about it. The Eye is someone who gets around. Someone who likes knowing things that other people don't know. Someone who enjoys being a secret watcher. The column's become incredibly popular. The Eye could have got a bit power-mad. And used cut-out letters for the note just to make them more scary, and harder to trace.'

I shook my head. 'It's crazy,' I said again.

'Okay,' said Nick with a shrug. 'Prove it.'

I leaned against the desk, struggling to find words. Liz came over to stand beside me.

'I agree with Elmo,' she said firmly. 'I don't believe that The Eye could write a poison-pen letter. The columns are clever and funny, but they're never nasty.'

Nick rolled his eyes. Tom looked uncomfortable. For a moment it looked as though Teen Power Inc. was going to split into two opposing sides. Then Sunny took a hand.

'There's no point in just arguing about this,' she said sensibly. 'We need to figure out who wrote that poison-pen letter.'

Nick looked down at the scribbled words on his notepad. 'We haven't got much to go on,' he said. 'One scrappy note.'

Richelle was perched on the edge of the desk, swinging her foot idly to study the shine on her shoe. She glanced up at him. 'Well then, I suppose we'd better try to get hold of some more,' she said.

We all turned to stare at her. 'What do you mean?' Liz asked, looking puzzled.

Richelle shrugged. 'What I said. Poison-pen writers hardly ever stop with just one victim, do they? In all the stories I've ever read they don't, anyway. So other people have probably had notes as well.'

That's typical of Richelle. She has a habit of saying things that are totally obvious—except that somehow nobody else has managed to think of them.

'She's right,' Sunny said to me.

'Yes, but how do we track down the other letters?' Tom objected. 'We can hardly put an ad in the *Pen*, saying, "Write to us and tell us all the dirty gossip that The Eye's been spreading about you." Nobody in their right mind would answer.'

'Mrs Flower told us about *her* letter,' Liz pointed out.

'Mrs Flower's a very up-front sort of person, though,' I reminded her. 'And she works for the *Pen*, too. She knows Dad and everything. Most people would be ashamed of the things that the letters said about them, so they'd keep it to themselves. They'd just lie awake at night, worrying about it and wondering what was going to happen next.'

Liz shivered, but Nick jumped up. 'That's it,' he said abruptly. 'If we want to find more poison-pen victims, we need to check around for people who are upset and miserable, and not their usual selves.'

Liz, Tom and I looked at each other.

'Sam Frean!' we all said together.

Dad was looking very confused. 'Where are you going? Who's Sam Frean?' he called out to us, as we made for the door.

'Sam Frean, the butcher,' I yelled back. 'He's victim number two. You wait and see.'

Ten minutes later we were knocking on the window of the butcher's shop in Raven Hill Mall. It was after closing time, but we could see Sam Frean sitting at the back of the shop bent over some account books. He glanced in our direction and hastily looked away again.

Tom rapped his knuckles even more sharply against the glass. When Sam turned around, he started mouthing words at him, waving his hands dramatically. In the end the butcher pulled off his glasses, pushed back his chair and came over to unlock the door, frowning thunderously.

Nick had decided to take the direct approach. As soon as the door opened he looked straight into Sam Frean's eyes. 'We know about the letter you got,' he said. 'Could we see it, please?'

'Letter?' the butcher blustered, backing away. 'What letter?'

We followed him inside. You could see by the way he was acting that our hunch had been right.

'The words are cut out of newspaper,' Liz said gently, waving Nick aside. 'The note's signed "The Eye".'

Normally Sam Frean was round and rosy-cheeked, but all of a sudden he looked incredibly sickly and pale.

45

'I don't know what you're talking about,' he croaked desperately. 'Go away and leave me alone.'

'Sam, listen, you're not the only one to have got a letter,' Liz said, putting her hand on his arm. 'And we're not trying to blackmail you or anything. We just want to help. Elmo is the son of the man who runs the *Pen*. His father's terribly worried about all this. Please let us see the note. Please!'

Sam stared at her for a long moment. 'Oh, all right,' he said finally. 'What have I got to lose? If this monster's telling the truth, everybody will know about me soon anyway.'

He went back to the desk where he'd been working and pulled out two sheets of paper that had been hidden under the bills.

'There you are,' he said, shoving them into Liz's hand. 'They came to my home address but I keep them here, so my family won't find them.'

The first letter looked exactly the same as Mrs Flower's. Only the words were different:

THE EYE KNOWS ALL ABOUT YOU, YOU STUPID, GREEDY JERK. SOON EVERYONE WILL. SERVES YOU RIGHT.

The second letter read:

YOU CAN FOOL MOST PEOPLE BUT NOT ME. SOON I WILL BE SPREADING THE WORD. WAIT FOR IT.

Both of them were signed with The Eye signature, cut out of the *Pen*.

I gazed at the letters, feeling a bit sick. I couldn't understand why anyone would want to do a freaky thing like that. And I couldn't understand why the poison-pen writer was borrowing The Eye's name.

'Sam, these are *awful*,' murmured Liz. 'Why didn't you tell someone about them?'

Sam stared at her with a haunted expression. 'I didn't want anyone to know,' he muttered. 'And it was so—weird, Liz. How did The Eye find out? Nobody knew. Nobody but me.'

He rambled on like that for a while, but at last he admitted that for a few months during the year before, he'd been putting mutton into the lamb mince, because times were hard and mutton was cheaper than lamb.

'But why not?' he said defensively, pounding his fist against his palm. 'People liked it. The mutton added a bit of flavour. As a matter of fact, I sold more lamb mince than I ever had before—and at a good price too.'

'Then why are you so worried?' Sunny asked practically and he collapsed like a burst balloon.

'Because I shouldn't have done it,' he said in a small voice. 'It's caught up with me now. I've always had a good reputation, but The Eye's going to start a hate campaign against me and everybody'll think that I've been cheating them all the time. I haven't, though. I just slipped up the once, that's all.'

'People won't necessarily believe what they hear.

47

Most people don't think much of poison-pen letter writers, Sam,' Liz soothed.

'In general, no,' Sam sighed. 'But The Eye's different. People respect that column. They believe every word of it.'

'Yes, but The Eye who writes the column may not be the same person as The Eye who writes the poison-pen letters,' I pointed out.

'Here we go,' muttered Nick.

Sam just looked bewildered. It had obviously never occurred to him that the notes could have come from anyone but the real Eye.

Nick looked wistfully at the letters in Liz's hand.

'Do you want these back, Sam?' he asked, 'or can we keep them?'

'You take them if you want,' Sam growled. 'Just don't show them to anyone else, all right? I'll be glad to get them out of the shop. They make me sick every time I look at them. I just couldn't bring myself to burn them, somehow.'

Nick asked him a few more questions about the envelope and the stamp, and then we left.

Sam called out after us as we walked away. 'You tell your Dad to sack The Eye, Elmo,' he shouted. 'You tell him from me!'

As we walked back up the Mall, Nick weighed the letters thoughtfully in his hand. 'We really should take these to the police, you know,' he said.

'Nick!' Liz exclaimed, looking horrified, 'how can

48

you say that? We promised Sam we wouldn't show them to anyone.'

Nick enjoys shocking Liz. He grinned at her outraged face.

'Oh well, I don't suppose the cops'd find much in the way of fingerprints, anyhow,' he drawled. 'The Eye obviously isn't stupid, and probably watches the same TV programs as we do. Still, at least we've seen two sets of the letters now. That ought to be useful.'

'How?' Richelle asked with a blank, blue-eyed stare. 'As far as I can see, we aren't any further on than we were before.'

'Oh, it all adds up,' Nick said, waving his hand airily. 'Every little bit of information helps.'

Richelle didn't look convinced. And I must say I wasn't feeling too confident myself. All we'd really found out was that we'd been right about there being more than one poison-pen victim. Sam Frean was as upset and worried as Mrs Flower was. And there might be other people in the same position. All of them thinking they were being threatened by The Eye.

It was dreadful, I thought. We had to track down Poison Pen, whoever he or she was. Because quite apart from the misery being caused to people like Sam Frean and Mrs Flower, this whole business could really hurt the *Pen*.

If this story leaked out, then everyone would be convinced that The Eye was a cruel, cowardly sneak who delighted in making other people miserable.

49

Then, at best, Dad would have to drop the most popular column in the paper. And, at the worst, people might start thinking the *Pen* was Public Enemy Number 1 for using the Eye column in the first place.

So I really didn't have any choice. Poison Pen had to be found and unmasked. And quickly.

8

Brainwave

The others went home after that, and I went back to the Pen. I didn't think about the mystery for a while. I helped Dad with a few things, then we had fish and chips, like we usually did when we worked late. But after that he went back into his office and I was left alone to do my homework.

That's when I started thinking about Poison Pen again. And as I thought, I became more and more convinced that if there were two victims, there could easily be more.

Who did I know who had been acting strangely lately?

Well, Stephen Spiers had been crabby and edgy for a week or two. But that was just because he was jealous of The Eye, I was sure. And Liz's mum had been very tense and upset—but that was because she couldn't forget about the bank robbery.

Then suddenly I had a brainwave. I rushed to the phone and dialled Liz's number. She picked up the phone straightaway.

'Oh, hi, Elmo,' she said. 'How amazing. I was just about to call you.'

'Liz, I've thought of another person who might be getting letters from Poison Pen,' I gabbled. 'You'll never guess who it is.'

'I bet I will,' she said. 'Ms Adair.'

There was silence for a few seconds, and then we both burst out laughing.

'Great minds think alike,' Liz said cheerfully. 'I just worked it out, and I was about to pick up the phone to call you, when it rang. Listen, Elmo, let's meet before school and try to speak to Ms Adair first thing. Okay? If we're right, and we can tell her other people have had letters, and everything, she might decide not to leave after all. Wouldn't that be great?'

I agreed. 'Plus,' I reminded her, 'the more we know about the poison-pen letters, the bigger our chances are of finding out who's writing them.'

After Liz hung up I sat back with my hands behind my head and felt pleased. We're closing in on you, Poison Pen, I thought. We're tracking you down. And when we catch you, you'll be sorry you tried to use the *Pen* for your nasty work. You wait!

❂

The next morning Liz and I met as planned and raced to the English teachers' staff room, determined to corner Ms Adair. But it turned out to be harder than we'd thought.

When Ms Adair came out and saw us waiting outside, she ducked back inside and refused to come out till after we'd had to go to our first class. She did the same thing at recess.

We'd told the others about it by this time, and we all tried to catch her after our English class just before lunchtime. But she was too fast for us. She was out the door and off to the staff room before we'd even packed up our books.

'She doesn't want to talk to us,' Liz said while we gloomily ate our lunch. 'We're just hassling her, and she's got enough troubles. Maybe we ought to stop chasing her around. We don't *know* she's had a poison-pen letter.'

'Of course we do,' Nick said scornfully. 'I don't know why I didn't see before. It was staring us in the face. Remember how she went crazy yesterday just because Robbie was reading The Eye's column? Why would she do that—unless she was getting nasty letters signed "The Eye"?'

'Well we can't sort it out with her privately while she's running away from us,' said Sunny. 'And we can't hit her with it while other people are listening, can we, Nick? That wouldn't be fair.'

'Um—I've got an idea,' I put in. 'I think it'll work, too. What about if we . . .'

Ms Adair hurried out of school that afternoon, looking pale and tired. Her shoulders were slumped and her eyes were red-rimmed behind her tortoiseshell glasses. As she turned into the car park, she stopped short in surprise. Six of her students were lined up beside her old Toyota, watching her steadily.

'What are you doing here?' she demanded. 'Get away from my car at once!' She looked near to tears.

'Ms Adair, we need to talk to you,' Liz said earnestly. 'You've been getting horrible anonymous letters, haven't you?'

The teacher's face went even whiter than before. 'No,' she said tensely. 'No, of course not. Why would you ask me a thing like that, out of the blue?'

'Because you've been really tense and worried,' I told her. 'And because you freaked when you caught sight of The Eye's column in the *Pen*.'

Ms Adair tried to laugh. 'Honestly, Elmo! I always knew you had a good imagination, but I didn't realise you'd started making up fairytales in your spare time. What a ridiculous story. Now please, move away from my car. Now!'

'Ms Adair, you're not the only one,' Nick said urgently. 'Look!'

He whisked Sam Frean's letters out of his notebook and pointed at the signatures. Ms Adair took one look, gasped and started to shake uncontrollably.

'Come on, Ms Adair,' Sunny said calmly. 'Why don't you tell us about it? It's all right. Really. You're the third person we've found who's had letters like these.'

'We've got to find out who's writing them,' I pleaded.

'We've *got* to!'

Ms Adair sat down abruptly on the bonnet of the car, holding her head in her hands. 'All right,' she said in a muffled voice. 'What's the point in denying it, anyway? Yes, someone has been sending me those foul letters. They've been making my life a misery for weeks.'

Once she started talking, Ms Adair couldn't stop. She'd been keeping her feelings bottled up inside and now everything came pouring out in a rush. Like Sam Frean, she seemed to be glad to have the chance to tell the whole story.

'I've had three letters,' she said. 'When the first one arrived, I just threw it away. But then, after the second letter, I began to get really worried. And by the time the third letter came, I was a nervous wreck.'

'Have you still got the second two?' I asked, crossing my fingers.

She nodded miserably. 'Have a look at them, if you like,' she said. 'Nothing matters any more.'

She fished around in her enormous handbag and brought out two sheets of notepaper. While Nick copied the letters down, asking his usual questions about the postmarks and envelopes, the rest of us studied the familiar pattern of words cut out of a newspaper and pasted together.

The first letter read:

THE EYE KNOWS YOUR NASTY LITTLE SECRET. SOON EVERYONE WILL. SERVES YOU RIGHT.

And the second was no better:

> WAIT TILL EVERYONE FINDS OUT WHAT YOU ARE REALLY LIKE. YOU WON'T BE SO POPULAR THEN.

'It's the hate in the letters that's so unbearable,' Ms Adair said softly. 'I keep looking at everyone I know and wondering who dislikes me that much. In a way, it's a relief to find out that other people have been receiving the letters as well.'

She drew a shuddering breath. 'I'm sorry for them, of course, but I'm glad to know that I'm not the only one. The terrifying question is, how does The Eye find these things out about people? I wouldn't have thought anyone here would have known about . . .' Her voice trailed off.

'So what the letters say is true?' I asked bluntly. I knew I wasn't being very tactful, but by now I just wanted to find out everything I could.

Ms Adair twisted her hands together and looked up at me with a face full of sadness and pain. 'Just about everyone's got something to hide, Elmo,' she said finally. 'I'm no different. It isn't anybody else's business—or at least, it shouldn't be. Some things are meant to be kept private.'

That was all she'd tell us. She just kept repeating that she didn't understand how The Eye could have found out about her.

'I don't think The Eye is responsible for the letters,' I said stubbornly. 'You've read the column in the *Pen*, so you know there isn't anything spiteful in it. And yet the poison-pen writer has made at least three people absolutely miserable. Surely that proves that the letters and the column are written by two different people.'

Ms Adair shrugged hopelessly. 'You'd think so. But The Eye's obviously someone who loves secrets—the whole column's full of secrets and gossip. And maybe secrets you can print aren't enough fun for The Eye any more. Maybe dangerous secrets are more appealing. Things that people are scared will get around. Maybe The Eye likes to have that sort of power.'

'That's horrible,' shuddered Liz.

'It's wicked,' Ms Adair said quietly. 'And it's terrifying. At times like these, I almost wish I still went to church.'

She sighed again and held out her hand. Nick obediently passed the letters to her.

'Well,' she murmured, with a touch of her old humour, 'can I go home now, do you think? Or was there something else you wanted?'

'We—we think you ought to change your mind about leaving,' stammered Liz. 'We'll all miss you—very much—if you go.'

Sunny, Tom and I muttered our agreement.

Ms Adair bit her lip and bowed her head. 'It's nice of you to say that,' she murmured. 'Thanks.'

We glanced at each other and moved away from her car, but all of a sudden Richelle took a step forward.

'There's just one other thing,' she said seriously. 'It's about your glasses, Ms Adair. When I was at the optometrist's, I noticed a pair with really thin gold frames.

I mean, I wouldn't want them for myself, of course. But I reckon *you* ought to try something like that. They'd suit you much better than those thick brown ones, anyway.'

Sunny and Liz groaned quietly, but for the first time in ages, I saw Ms Adair's mouth twitch into a smile.

'Thank you, Richelle,' she said politely. 'It's very kind of you to have mentioned it. I'll certainly think about it. As soon as I've got a few other things off my mind.'

9

Another victim

The gang had to split up after that. Liz was going home to spend time with her mother again. Sunny had a tae-kwon-do session. I was needed at the *Pen*, because we went to press that night. And it was Nick and Richelle's turn to visit the dreaded Mrs Drisk-Haskell.

But Tom walked part of the way to the *Pen* with me and of course we talked about Ms Adair.

'She was really upset,' he kept saying, looking upset himself at the memory. Although you never see that side of him in public, Tom is much more sensitive than he lets on. I often think that he uses jokes and clowning around as a big cover up.

We stopped at a take-away shop so that Tom could buy some chips and a hamburger. Upset or not, he was still hungry. I like food myself, but I can never understand how Tom can fit in everything he does. Maybe it's because he's so tall.

We walked on, sharing the chips. They tasted good,

I must say. I licked my salty fingers, and went on talking.

'The only trouble is, we didn't really find out anything new from Ms Adair's letters,' I said. 'They were exactly the same as the others. They didn't give us any extra clues to Poison Pen's identity.'

'Not yet, anyway,' mumbled Tom, with his mouth full of hamburger. 'But like Nick says, it all adds up.' For a moment he looked annoyed to find himself quoting Nick, but then he laughed. 'Even Nick has to be right some of the time,' he added.

I nodded. 'I guess we should try to track down some more of Poison Pen's victims,' I said. 'If there *are* any more.'

'We have to look for people who are behaving strangely,' said Tom. 'Well, more strangely than usual, I mean. People who seem worried, or nervous, or . . .'

It struck me like a thunderbolt. I swung around to him and snapped my fingers. He stared at me in surprise.

'Mr Richardson!' I exclaimed.

'Mr *Richardson*? Who's he?'

'This guy I met at the optometrist's yesterday. He overheard Nick say that I worked at the *Pen*. He cornered me afterwards. After the others had gone. He wanted to know who The Eye was. He offered me fifty dollars—*fifty*—to tell him who The Eye was. *He* acted nervous, Tom. It didn't make sense to me at the time, but I'll bet it was because he's been getting anonymous letters.'

Tom stuffed the last of his hamburger into his

mouth in excitement. 'Great!' he said, chewing madly. 'Listen, we've got to track him down again. Would your optometrist give us his phone number, do you reckon?'

'No need,' I said triumphantly. 'He gave me his home phone number. And he told me to ring him any night after six.'

'He won't tell you anything over the phone,' Tom warned me. 'Remember, we had to work quite hard on Sam and Ms Adair before they'd admit anything. I reckon you ought to ask this guy to meet you somewhere. And the rest of us will come along too, just in case he turns nasty.'

'Okay then, I'll ring him tonight and arrange a meeting for tomorrow.'

'Great!' Tom said again, looking very pleased. 'Maybe this time we'll find out something that will really help.'

He said goodbye, then, and hurried off home. I guess he was still hungry. I went on to the *Pen*.

When I arrived the office was in a total uproar, just like it always is on press night. Zim was racing around, doing his best to be in six places at once. Miss Moss was shouting frantically into the phone. Stephen Spiers was crouched in a corner with yellow ear-plugs stuffed into his ears, trying to write a last-minute story.

I've helped at the *Pen* for ages now, so I knew exactly what needed doing. Within ten seconds of walking in the door I was running around with proofs and messages and getting orders for tea and coffee.

'Here's a proof of The Eye's column,' Dad called out to me. 'Could you check it through, Elmo? I've decided to run it as usual.'

'Good,' I said, taking the page from him.

Dad shrugged. 'Mrs Flower won't be too pleased with me,' he said. 'But I don't see what else I can do. If I don't run it I'll have to give some sort of explanation— otherwise I'll get a bucket of complaints. I'm still bothered about it, though. I'll need to think about it again next week.'

I glanced at the bottom of the column. There was The Eye's name, just as I'd seen it on all the anonymous letters. Normally I was pleased to see a new Eye column in print, but this time I just felt sick.

Still, at least I'd come up with another way to learn a bit more about the poison-pen writer. I waited until after six and then I found a phone that nobody was using. Mr Richardson answered straightaway, sounding very keen to talk, but I just told him to meet me outside the *Pen* at 6.15 the following evening.

'Can't you tell me anything now?' he begged. 'You needn't worry about the money. I'll make sure you get it.'

'Sorry, Mr Richardson. See you at 6.15 tomorrow night,' I said curtly and hung up.

I stood there frowning at the phone for a minute or two. Mr Richardson had sounded really desperate. I was certain that he was another Poison Pen victim, and I felt as bad as he did about having to wait so long till we could talk.

But I knew Tom was right. It wouldn't be a good idea to tackle the man alone. And if we were going to get any information from him, we had to see him face to face.

❁

Next morning I had to get up early. Delivering the *Pen* around Raven Hill is one of Teen Power's regular weekly jobs. I told the others about the meeting with Mr Richardson, but we didn't have much time to talk about it. We couldn't discuss it after school either, because Richelle was going to have her eyes tested and Liz and I were racing off to Mrs Drisk-Haskell's place.

'See you at the *Pen* later on,' Tom called after us as we hurried through the school gates. 'Let's meet up at six, so we can have a chance to talk before Mr Richardson gets there.'

When Liz and I arrived at Mrs Drisk-Haskell's place, the postman was trying to stuff four letters into the tiny little ornamental mailbox.

'Don't worry,' Liz told him in her usual friendly way. 'We'll take those for you.' He gave the letters to us with a grunt, and we carried them up to the house, leaving them on a polished table in the hall.

Mrs Drisk-Haskell was as full of herself as ever. Liz was wearing a blue jacket, so she told us a long story about how she'd been dressed in blue on the day she first met Reg. And she asked me several gracious questions about the *Pen*, although she still seemed to have to stop herself shuddering every time she looked at my hair or my clothes.

After a while she went away, leaving Liz and me to make a start on the dusting and vacuuming. I was brushing a cobweb from a huge portrait of Reg when Mrs Drisk-Haskell appeared in the doorway. Her face was ashen and she was tugging so hard at her string of pearls that I was afraid she might break them.

'That's enough,' she said sharply. 'You can leave now and you needn't bother to come back. Especially you, young man. I never want to see you here again!'

She gave me a withering look and stood over us while we gathered up our bag of cleaning equipment. As we scuttled down the steps, Liz turned to me with a comical expression of dismay.

'What happened?' she asked, when we were standing in the drive. 'What did we do?'

I shrugged. 'Don't ask me. Maybe she's a nut-case. Maybe she thought we stole something, like Mrs Flower.'

'No, that can't be it,' Liz objected. 'We weren't there for long enough. Maybe she heard some sort of nasty gossip about us, though. Maybe one of her posh friends rang up and—'

I was already shaking my head. 'I didn't hear the phone. No-one rang the front door bell, either. We just must have done something she didn't like.'

'But we didn't do *anything*!' exclaimed Liz, getting all worked up at the unfairness of it all. 'We arrived on time. We listened politely to her boring story. We even brought in her mail for her.'

Those letters! Excitement stabbed at me. 'The mail!' I shouted. 'That's it. Liz! Mrs Drisk-Haskell got a letter. A letter signed by The Eye. No wonder she suddenly got angry. And with me, especially. She probably thinks I'm in on the whole business, because I work at the *Pen*.'

'Of course!' Liz's irritation vanished and she clapped her hands. 'But what on earth could The Eye be writing to Mrs Drisk-Haskell about? She's so highly respected and everything. She keeps telling us so.'

'Like Ms Adair says, almost everyone's got something to hide,' I said grimly. 'Come on.'

We charged back up the steps and rang the bell. Mrs Drisk-Haskell came to the door looking worried and tense. Of course, when she saw us she tried to shut the door again, but I wriggled past her into the hall, dragging Liz with me.

'What do you think you're doing?' Mrs Drisk-Haskell hissed, furiously angry. 'How dare you come bursting in here? Get out!'

Liz was pink with embarrassment, but I was determined.

'Mrs Drisk-Haskell, I'm sorry, but this is really important,' I said. 'The letter you just opened. It was a poison-pen letter, wasn't it? Signed "The Eye".'

Mrs Drisk-Haskell drew herself up and gazed at me haughtily. 'I haven't the faintest idea of what you're talking about,' she snapped.

My eyes darted to the polished table. Three opened letters lay there. The fourth was nowhere to be seen, but in the wastepaper basket under the table was a brown envelope, and some paper that had been ripped and crumpled.

Before Mrs Drisk-Haskell could do anything to stop me, I dived for the basket. As I pulled out some of the screwed-up scraps of paper and smoothed them out I saw the tell-tale jigsaw of words cut from newspaper. And the signature. The Eye. I had found another poison-pen letter.

Mrs Drisk-Haskell was totally crushed. She didn't even try to bluster. She just started to cry big fat tears that made pale tracks through the blusher on her cheeks.

'How could you?' she choked. Then she turned, and ran for the bathroom.

Liz and I emptied the scraps out of the wastepaper basket and started to piece them together on the table. Within a few minutes we found ourselves staring down at Poison Pen's latest message:

YOU THINK YOU ARE SAFE. BUT THE EYE SEES EVERYTHING. SOON ALL YOUR FRIENDS WILL FIND OUT WHAT A NASTY PIECE OF WORK YOU REALLY ARE.

There were footsteps behind us. When we turned

around, Mrs Drisk-Haskell was standing there. She'd tried to repair her makeup, but she still looked very bedraggled, and her eyes were puffy and watery.

'Will you please go?' she said in a trembling voice.

'Mrs Drisk-Haskell, we're sorry to upset you,' Liz said gently. 'We're sorry we were so rude before. But lots of people around Raven Hill have been getting letters like this. We found out sort of by accident. And Elmo especially wants to find out who's sending them. People think they've got something to do with the *Pen*, because they're signed "The Eye".'

'Well, of course they do!' shrilled Mrs Drisk-Haskell, turning furious, red-rimmed eyes on me. 'What else are they supposed to think?'

I bit my lip. There wasn't much of an answer to that one.

Mrs Drisk-Haskell turned away, and her shoulders slumped. 'I don't understand how this could have happened,' she whispered, clutching at her pearls. 'It was so long ago. How could anybody know about it?'

She wandered off into the living room. After a moment we followed, and found her standing under the portrait of Reg Drisk-Haskell.

'So it's going to come out at last,' she murmured. 'After all these years.' She looked up at the portrait of her husband, and went on speaking. It was as if she was talking to him, not to us at all.

'These days everybody knows me as Jeanette Drisk-Haskell,' she began. 'But when I was a girl, I was just

67

plain Janet Greeb. My family lived on a little farm. We were terribly poor. The farm didn't make enough to keep us all. I had to leave school at fourteen and take a job in a local factory—plucking chickens.'

Liz glanced at me, her face a mixture of surprise and sympathy.

'After a few years of that, I ran away to the city and worked as a waitress,' Mrs Drisk-Haskell said. 'That's how I met Reg, carrying plates to his table in my blue uniform. He fell in love with me on the spot and we were married two weeks later. It was like a fairytale.'

A tiny smile trembled on her lips. Then she shook her head.

'I told him I was an orphan. I was so ashamed of my family. I didn't want him to meet them. I wanted to forget that I'd ever been poor. I wrote to my mother and father and told them I was being married and starting a new life overseas, so they shouldn't try to find me. And I never contacted them again.'

She buried her face in her hands with a muffled sob.

'You were very young,' whispered kind-hearted Liz.

'That's no excuse,' Mrs Drisk-Haskell said fiercely. 'It was wrong. A terrible thing to do. Now both my parents are dead and I can never ask them to forgive me. Never.'

She lifted her head and stared directly at us. For the first time I could see why Reg had liked her so much. She wasn't making any excuses for herself. I had to admire her for that.

'It was wicked,' she said in a low voice. 'I must have hurt my family very badly. And now The Eye has somehow found out about everything and I'm going to be punished for it. At last.'

10

Confusion

As we left Mrs Drisk-Haskell's house for the second time, Liz and I were still trying to take in what we'd just heard.

'You know, Elmo, I would have laughed if anyone had said that Mrs Drisk-Haskell might be one of Poison Pen's victims,' Liz burst out at last. 'She always seemed so confident and sure of herself.'

'Yes, but that's why Poison Pen was able to get to her,' I pointed out. 'She wanted to impress Reg and her fancy new friends. So she told a lie—and let herself in for a whole lot of misery.'

'I feel sorry for her, though,' Liz said sadly. 'The person who's writing those letters must be very hard and cruel. Oh Elmo, I hope The Eye *isn't* the anonymous letter writer. You still believe that The Eye and Poison Pen are two separate people, don't you?'

'Yes,' I told her firmly. 'I can't prove it yet, but we'll figure out the truth in the end. I know we will.'

We went on to the *Pen* office, where we found Tom and Sunny and Nick waiting for us. While Liz told them about what had happened with Mrs Drisk-Haskell, I took out the envelope and torn up letter and stuck the pieces together again.

When I'd finished, Nick came over to have a look. He got out Sam Frean's letters and the copies he'd made of Poison Pen's letters to Mrs Flower and Ms Adair.

'Mr Richardson isn't supposed to turn up for a while yet,' he said. 'Why don't we have a really serious go at solving the problem?'

Thursday is a quiet day at the *Pen*, so we had the big back room to ourselves by now.

We laid out the letters in a row on one of the desks and started to prowl around them, frowning to ourselves as we tried to figure out what they could tell us.

'Okay, somebody has to state the obvious,' Tom began. 'It might as well be me—seeing that Richelle hasn't arrived yet. Here goes. Poison Pen obviously has some sort of connection with Ms Adair, Mrs Flower, Mrs Drisk-Haskell, Sam Frean and possibly this mysterious Mr Richardson. I mean, you don't send anonymous letters to people you don't know, right?'

'That's pretty basic, for sure,' Nick jeered. Then he thought about it for a moment. 'But it's interesting too, in a way,' he admitted, 'because they're such a varied group of people. It's hard to see how they all link up.'

'*We* know all of them,' Tom said with a grin.

'That doesn't get us very far,' muttered Sunny.

'Well, what can we tell from these letters?' frowned Nick.

'The Eye is someone who's in a position to find out other people's secrets,' Tom said promptly.

'Stop calling this person The Eye!' I snapped. 'It's not fair. It's—'

'Okay, okay,' Nick sighed. 'Poison Pen can find out other people's secrets, then. What else can we work out?'

'Poison Pen dislikes all the people who've got letters, and wants to frighten them,' Liz put in.

'Okay,' Nick muttered, scribbling away in his notebook. 'Now we're getting somewhere. I'll tell you another thing too. Poison Pen has a typewriter. All the addresses on the envelopes have been typed.'

'Hey, and that reminds me of something else,' I said suddenly. 'Poison Pen knows all the victims' addresses. The letters to Sam Frean and Ms Adair arrived at their homes, remember, not at the butcher's shop or the school.'

'That doesn't prove anything,' Sunny objected. 'Poison Pen could easily have got their addresses out of the phone book.'

'Wrong,' I told her. 'Mrs Drisk-Haskell has an unlisted phone number, so the phone book is out. Poison Pen knows the victims better than that.'

Tom peered closely at the letters and his eyes widened. 'Listen, I've thought of another clue. Poison Pen must have plenty of spare time and privacy. It would have taken a long time to put those letters together, because of all the cutting and pasting.'

'That's right,' I said. 'And, listen, why would someone like The Eye bother with all that? The Eye's stuff is typed on a computer. We get the copy every week—you've seen it. Why would The Eye go to so much trouble on poison-pen letters, and not bother to disguise his copy?'

'Hmm,' Nick said thoughtfully. 'That's an interesting point. Maybe I was wrong about The Eye, after all. Come to think of it, you've raised another interesting point as well, Elmo. Poison Pen has a typewriter but he or she only uses it for the envelopes, not for the actual notes. Why? It doesn't make sense.'

'Yes, it does,' Tom said immediately, grabbing at the chance to contradict Nick. 'What if Poison Pen is using *somebody else*'s typewriter? A work typewriter, for example, or one in a typewriter shop. Typing a quick name and address is one thing. Typing a whole note, even a short note, is different.'

Liz nodded excitedly. 'Just imagine what would happen if someone walked past and read a bit of the letter. Poison Pen simply couldn't risk it.'

'Fair enough,' Nick agreed. 'But why type the envelope at all, in that case?'

I narrowed my eyes and studied Mrs Drisk-Haskell's envelope carefully. 'It looks like an ordinary business letter,' I commented. 'Maybe that's the answer. If Poison Pen used bits of cut out newspaper for the addresses, the victims would start to feel suspicious before they even opened the letters. It wouldn't work, especially if you wanted to frighten somebody two or three times.'

'And handwriting, even block printing, would be too dangerous, because police experts can identify handwriting styles,' Nick added. 'Okay, that explains the envelopes. Now let's go back to where we started. Who knows all the victims? And who could find out their secrets?'

'Doctors know a lot of secrets about people,' Liz said with a sidelong glance at Sunny. 'Do all of those people go to the same doctor?'

'No,' Sunny said definitely. 'Sam Frean goes to my mother—he always tries to get free advice about his varicose veins every time she's in there buying meat. And we know that Mrs Drisk-Haskell *isn't* one of Mum's patients, because she said Reg insisted on sending her to a specialist in the city.'

'Who else is in the same position as a doctor, then?' I asked. 'How about a priest?'

'Elmo!' Liz exclaimed. 'A priest wouldn't write anonymous letters.'

Nick raised one eyebrow and glanced at her cynically. 'What a nice person you are, Liz,' he drawled. 'So sweet and innocent.'

Liz looked furious.

'Break it up, you two,' Tom chipped in hastily. 'A priest's out anyway. Ms Adair made it pretty clear that she hadn't been near a church in years.'

'So doctors are out and priests are out,' I mused. 'Are there any other jobs that involve hearing people's secrets?'

'Counsellors or psychologists,' Liz suggested and Nick laughed.

'We could check it out, but I don't think it's very likely. I can't see Mrs Flower going to any kind of counsellor. Ms Adair might possibly be interested in talking to someone about her innermost thoughts, but not Mrs Drisk-Haskell. I bet she doesn't even *have* any innermost thoughts.'

Liz looked as though she was about to leap to Mrs Drisk-Haskell's defence. Luckily, at that moment Sunny had another thought.

'Listen, I'm going off on a completely different tack here, but how about cleaners?' she suggested. 'Cleaners tidy desks and open cupboards and empty wastepaper baskets. They must learn an awful lot about the people they work for.'

'Yes, but the only cleaner we've heard about so far is Mrs Flower and she actually *had* one of the poison-pen letters,' I pointed out.

Nick's eyes gleamed. 'Maybe she sent a note to herself, to throw everyone off the track,' he said. 'After all, she fits our description of Poison Pen pretty closely. She could have typed those envelopes on one of the old typewriters at the *Pen*.'

'Rubbish!' I snapped. 'You saw Mrs Flower's face when she was yelling at Dad about The Eye. She was really upset, Nick. She definitely wasn't faking it.'

'I don't think you can be so sure about that,' Nick insisted. 'If Mrs Flower is Poison Pen, then she enjoys fooling people. She would've got a kick out of putting on a big act.'

'Don't judge other people by yourself,' Tom cut in. 'Mrs Flower is the honest, up-front sort. You wouldn't understand, Nick.'

While Tom and Nick went on arguing about Mrs Flower, I sidled off and started to test all the typewriters in the *Pen* office, to see if I could find one that looked as though it might have been used to type the poison-pen envelopes. I hadn't quite finished when the door flew open and Richelle came hurtling in.

'Guess *what*?' she announced, looking thrilled. 'I don't need reading glasses, after all. Ms Salamandi says I just have to do eye exercises every day. She gave me this sheet of them to follow. They're not hard at all.'

'Wow, that's exciting news,' Tom said sarcastically. 'You've really made my day.'

Richelle took no notice of him. 'I'll show you,' she said to Liz. She perched on the desk and started fossicking around in her bag. 'Oh, by the way, there's a man in a suit hanging round outside,' she added absent-mindedly.

I checked my watch. 'It's only ten to six. If it is Mr Richardson, then he's early.'

'Good, that means he must be nervous,' Nick commented. 'Let's make him wait for a bit longer, to soften him up. Besides, I want to see whether Richelle's got any useful suggestions. Here, Richelle, take a look at my notebook. I've jotted down all the points we've been discussing.'

Richelle reluctantly stopped looking in her bag, and glanced at Nick's notes.

'Well, you can forget about Mrs Flower,' she said straightaway. 'She couldn't possibly be Poison Pen. I went to her place once. She lives in a really tiny flat and she even shares a bedroom with her daughter. There's no way she could get enough privacy to stick those notes together.'

Nick looked disappointed. 'Okay, can you think of anyone else who might know other people's secrets?' he asked.

'A hairdresser,' Richelle said promptly, shaking back her own long blonde hair. 'Everyone always chats to hairdressers. I've overheard the most amazing things while I've been—'

'Forget it,' Sunny interrupted brusquely. 'If you can believe that Sam Frean and Mrs Drisk-Haskell go to the same hairdresser, you can believe anything.'

'There must be *something* that all the victims have in common,' Liz exclaimed.

'Well, there is,' Richelle said, opening her blue eyes wide.

We all turned to her at once, hoping that she was about to come out with another one of her brilliantly obvious remarks. Richelle blinked at us.

'They're all getting poison-pen letters, aren't they?' she said.

Liz groaned. 'Thanks, Richelle. That was incredibly helpful. Listen, why doesn't Elmo go outside and get this Mr Richardson now? I'm dying to hear what he has to say.'

11

Sorry, Mr Richardson

When I went out into the street, Mr Richardson was pacing up and down, looking very nervous. He spotted me straightaway and came striding towards me.

'I didn't realise you were in the office already,' he growled. 'You should have come and fetched me.'

'You're a bit early, Mr Richardson,' I said politely. 'I didn't dream you'd be so anxious—just about a bet.'

Ignoring his angry scowl, I swung away and led him through the reception area, down the corridor, and into the back room where the others were waiting. As I expected, Mr Richardson didn't look too pleased to see them. In fact, he looked furious. And when he noticed Liz, his face turned positively pale.

Liz seemed fairly uncomfortable as well. 'Oh, I didn't realise!' she exclaimed in surprise. She turned to the rest of us, obviously trying to pull herself together.

'Mr Richardson is Mum's boss at the bank,' she explained.

Mr Richardson nodded to her, making the best of it. 'Well, how's your mother getting on, Elizabeth?' he said in his hearty voice. 'I noticed that she had to leave early again yesterday.'

'Oh, she's fine,' Liz said hastily.

I shot her a look of sympathy, because I knew her mum was worried that she might get fired if she couldn't pull herself together soon.

'Listen, Mr Richardson, about The Eye . . .' I began, to get his attention away from Liz.

He jerked, and started to look nervous again. 'We won't talk about that now, I don't think,' he said hastily, glancing at the others. 'I told you this was—a private matter. And I'd prefer we kept it that way, if you don't mind.'

'The others know,' I said bluntly. I was feeling pretty nervous myself, but I couldn't see any point in messing around.

Mr Richardson's face turned a dull red. I pushed on.

'We want to ask you if you've had one or more poison-pen letters,' I said, watching him. 'Letters signed "The Eye".'

The man started to splutter. 'Don't be ridiculous,' he managed to say, after a moment.

Nick smiled at him lazily, like a cat who'd just stolen the cream. Then he unexpectedly took a step sideways, away from Zim's desk.

When Mr Richardson spotted the row of letters on the desk, his jaw dropped and his eyes bulged alarmingly.

He whipped out a white handkerchief and began to polish his thick glasses, controlling himself with an effort. It was obvious that he'd seen Poison Pen's style of letter-writing before. But it was equally obvious that he wasn't going to admit it.

'We'd like you to know that The Eye isn't responsible for the poison-pen letters, Mr Richardson,' I told him firmly. 'It's somebody else, using The Eye's name. Somebody who knows you and knows your address and knows a secret about you that most people don't. We're trying to track that person down. Can we see your letter?'

Instinctively Mr Richardson's hand flew to the breast pocket of his suit in a protective gesture.

'This is outrageous and insulting,' he shouted furiously. 'If anyone sent *me* one of those disgusting letters, I'd take it straight to the police. I don't have anything to hide, I can promise you that.'

He went on blustering at us until his face was purple with rage. Liz looked at him in alarm. Nick, Tom and Sunny whispered to each other.

'Get some water, Elmo,' hissed Sunny. 'A big glass of water.'

I dashed to the back of the room where the sink and coffee-making stuff was, and returned with a glass of water.

Sunny took it from me and held it out. 'Have some water, Mr Richardson,' she said calmly.

He waved her away impatiently.

And then a very strange thing happened. Sunny—

careful, sensible Sunny, such a whiz at gym, so clever and agile in everything she did—jumped backwards, fell over her own feet, and tipped the water all over the man's jacket.

Liz squealed, and Mr Richardson roared with rage.

'Oh,' squeaked Sunny. 'Oh, I'm terribly sorry. Oh, quick, get the jacket off and we'll dry it for you. Help me, Nick.'

She was already pulling the jacket off. The bank manager tried to protest, but she was too quick for him. In seconds she had whisked the jacket away and had passed it to Nick.

'There's a towel in the kitchen,' I said helpfully, but Nick went racing off in the direction of the toilets.

Mr Richardson stood there in his shirt sleeves, shivering and scowling at us. He didn't say another word. After what seemed ages Nick came back.

'About time!' The man snatched his jacket and put it on.

'Don't contact me again, you,' he snapped at me as he struggled into it. 'You can say goodbye to your fifty dollars. Stupid kid!'

He shot a furious look at Liz, who was trying to shrink back into the shadows, and stormed out of the room and back up the corridor. We heard the door slamming behind him as he left the building.

'How *embarrassing*!' moaned Richelle.

'Sunny, how *could* you let that happen, when you know Mum works for that man?' Liz wailed. Then she broke off and narrowed her eyes at Nick, Sunny and Tom.

'Hold on,' she said suspiciously. 'Why are the three of you looking so smug?'

'Because our plan worked,' Tom said gleefully. 'You did a terrific job, Sunny. I couldn't see how you were going to get the jacket off him, but you managed it brilliantly.'

'Oh, it was easy,' she said with a modest smile. 'I just dug my thumb into his shoulder blade to make him push his shoulders back. Tae-kwon-do teaches you lots of little tricks like that. You should try it.'

'I don't believe it,' Liz screamed. 'You actually threw water over my mother's boss *on purpose*, and then you *assaulted* him. Poor Mum's in enough trouble at the bank already, without this.'

'I don't think you need to worry about your mum,' Nick said coolly. 'Mr Richardson has other things on his mind. Like the letter I found in his breast pocket, for example.'

'Yes!' Tom punched the air in triumph. 'It was there! I knew it was. What did it say?'

'It looked just like the others, and it was signed "The Eye". It said: "You think you are so clever, but I know all about you. Soon everyone will. Then you will be in trouble. Serves you right."'

Nick has a great memory. He smiled at us, waiting for the applause, but Richelle just shrugged.

'Well, so what? That gets us exactly nowhere. All that childish, embarrassing performance was for nothing,' she said, with a toss of her head. 'That note's just like all the others. It doesn't tell us anything new. The fact is, it doesn't really say anything at all.'

I looked at her in amazement. All of a sudden my brain had gone into overdrive. I could feel a whole chain of ideas connecting up at incredible speed.

'Richelle, you're a genius,' I shouted.

She blinked at me. 'What did I say?'

'The note doesn't say anything,' I spluttered.

Nick sighed wearily. 'What are you on about, Zimmer?' he drawled.

'Don't you see?' I exclaimed. 'Richelle's absolutely right. The note doesn't say *anything*.'

12

'We've got it all wrong!'

Richelle wrinkled her forehead. 'I know I'm much smarter than people sometimes think,' she said. 'But this time I don't get it.'

'Me neither,' Tom put in.

I swung around and pointed to the row of letters on the desk. 'Go on, read through the messages again,' I said excitedly. 'None of them say anything special. They're just vaguely threatening, no more than that.'

The others scanned the letters quickly and looked up at me with puzzled frowns. I felt irritated with them for being so slow—but at the same time I also felt pleased to be the one who'd made the breakthrough.

'We've got it all wrong,' I told them. 'We've been looking for somebody who knows other people's secrets. But there's no proof in these letters that the person who wrote them actually knows anything at *all*.

There's nothing said here about Mrs Drisk-Haskell's past or Sam Frean's lamb mince, or Ms Adair's problem, whatever it is—or about Mrs Flower being a thief.'

'No, there's not,' frowned Nick. 'Why didn't I see that before?'

'None of us did.' Liz shook her head. 'Oh, we were so *stupid*.'

'Speak for yourself, Free,' said Tom, tilting his nose at her. 'Why should we see it? The people who got the letters didn't.'

'It's like that Sherlock Holmes story,' bubbled Liz, full of excitement. 'You know, in one of those stories it says that if you sent a note saying "Fly, all is known" to practically anyone, they'd pack their bags and run straightaway. Because most people have some kind of guilty secret.'

'I don't,' said Richelle, looking quite insulted.

'Oh no?' Liz asked straightaway. 'What about the time you lost your mum's jade ring? She still doesn't know about that, does she? And what about that time in kindergarten when you—?'

'Liz!' Richelle shrieked, blushing to the roots of her hair.

Liz flashed her a wicked grin.

Nick raised one eyebrow. 'It's true,' he said coolly. 'Most people have got at least one thing they feel guilty or embarrassed about.'

'One?' Tom boasted. 'I've got hundreds.'

'We've got it all wrong!'

'Even Elmo's probably got *something* to hide,' Sunny teased, giving me a sidelong glance.

I didn't say anything, but I had to work hard to stop myself from blushing as hotly as Richelle.

'Well, the point is,' said Nick, moving right along in case anyone's attention turned to him, 'all the people who got one of these letters did exactly what Sherlock Holmes said. They just jumped to the conclusion that The Eye, or Poison Pen, or whatever, knew their secret, and they panicked.'

'The thing is,' Liz put in slowly, 'this really makes the problem harder. Because now Poison Pen could be *anyone*. Anyone at all who knows these particular people and wants to make them unhappy.'

'But why *these* people?' puzzled Tom. 'They couldn't be more different. Some of them are rich and some of them are poor. They look different, they work at different jobs, they live in different parts of Raven Hill . . .'

'And I don't like any of them very much,' Richelle added, as if she was making a really useful contribution to the discussion.

'Aha! A confession at last,' frowned Tom, grabbing Nick's notebook and pretending to take notes. 'So, Ms Brinkley. You're finally coming clean and admitting that you're Poison Pen, are you?'

'Don't be stupid!' Richelle flicked back her hair impatiently. 'I just said that I don't like any of them much. I don't like those loud, pushy people. They're irritating.'

'Ms Adair isn't loud or pushy,' Liz objected. 'She's lovely.'

'Oh, you know what I mean,' Richelle said, making a face. 'She's always so smiling and cheerful and she acts as though everything's just great all the time. It gets on my nerves.'

'She's not smiling and cheerful now,' I said slowly. 'Nor is Sam Frean—and Sam's usually on top of the world.'

'Exactly,' Richelle said, as though I'd proved her point. 'It's so *irritating*. You'd think he was a famous actor or incredibly rich or something, instead of just being an ordinary old butcher.'

'Mrs Drisk-Haskell is really confident and pleased with herself too,' Sunny said thoughtfully. 'Or at least she was, until today.'

'As for Mrs Flower—it'd take a bulldozer to flatten her,' Tom remarked with a grin.

'A bulldozer—or an anonymous letter,' Nick added.

'And Mr Richardson is Mr Successful,' Liz told us. 'Mr Confident. Mr Superior. That's what Mum calls him. Although I can remember her saying that he'd been much quieter and more worried-looking lately. She put it down to the robbery, of course. She didn't know that he'd been getting anonymous letters.'

'You know, I think we've got it,' I said with rising excitement. 'What if Poison Pen's somebody who comes into contact with all these people and hates them just because they seem so happy and confident? Somebody who wants to take them down a peg and make them feel worried and miserable for a change.'

'That's awful!' protested Sunny.

'Maybe. But it makes sense,' Liz nodded. 'I read an article about poison-pen writers in a magazine once. Apparently, they're often really sad, lonely and insecure people. They're angry because nobody thinks they're important and they keep their feelings hidden all the time. So the letters are a way of getting their revenge. You know—a way of giving them power over other people.'

'It's very bad for you to keep your feelings bottled up,' Richelle put in knowledgeably.

'Well, no-one could accuse you of that, Richelle,' Tom joked. 'You're taking very good care of your mental health.'

Richelle hesitated, trying to work out whether he was insulting or complimenting her.

'Okay, it's time to review our data,' Liz said hastily. 'What've we got, Nick?'

He looked at his notebook. 'Up to the minute, this is what we know about the victims,' he said. 'They are: 1 People who Poison Pen knows; 2 People whose *addresses* Poison Pen knows; 3 People who are usually very happy and confident.'

'What about Poison Pen?' I asked.

'As far as Poison Pen is concerned, we know that

Poison Pen is: 1 Someone with access to a typewriter; 2 Someone with privacy at home; 3 Someone who knows all the victims; 4 Someone who has the victims' addresses; 5 Probably someone who is lonely and insecure and feels unimportant.'

'Too bad,' Tom said mischievously. 'That last item means that it can't be Richelle, after all.'

Richelle turned her back on him. She took her eye exercises out of their envelope and started rolling her eyes from side to side. It looked fairly weird, but she took it very seriously.

Tom crawled around in front of her and started imitating her, trying to make her laugh. But she wouldn't take any notice of him.

'Leave her alone, Tom,' groaned Liz. 'Don't be such a pain! Listen, just come back here and have another look at these letters.'

I was already looking. And I was thinking, too. I'd had an idea.

I opened my mouth to say something to the others, then closed it again. There was still something that didn't quite fit.

I stood there, looking at the gang. Liz and Tom were squabbling, Sunny was doing leg stretches against the desk, Nick was puzzling over his notebook and Richelle had switched from rolling her eyes sideways, to looking up and down. As far as they were concerned, the mystery was as deep as ever.

But the more I thought about it, the more I was

sure I had the answer. I just needed to check something out first.

13

Hot goss

When I arrived at Raven Hill High next morning, the place was really buzzing. Kids were gathered together in groups all over the place, talking excitedly. It was obvious that something unusual had happened.

I squeezed into the group around Carol Baxter. Carol is a born gossip. She knows everything that's going on at Raven Hill High and, what's more, she likes to pass the information on. I've always found her a reliable source.

'Okay, so she isn't leaving after all,' one of the kids was saying. 'But what's all this about her getting poison-pen letters?'

Of course then I really pricked up my ears.

Carol glanced around, to make sure she had everyone's attention. Then she bent forward. '*Apparently*, Adair's been getting all these anonymous letters,' she said in a hushed voice. 'From someone who knows this scandal about her. That's why she resigned—

because she was scared that the letter-writer would tell. But now for some reason she's made up her mind to get in first and tell everybody herself.'

'What scandal, what scandal?' asked Debbie Bray eagerly.

Carol bent forward even further. The whole circle bent with her. 'Well, what I heard,' she said, spinning the suspense out as far as possible, 'is that Adair was involved in a hit-and-run accident.'

'Ms *Adair*?' scoffed Walter Leu. 'I don't believe it.'

'Well, it's true,' Carol insisted. 'I heard old Lemon telling Staggers about it in the maths staff room only ten minutes ago. It was ages ago. Before Adair came to Raven Hill. When she'd just got out of college. She was teaching in this little country town. One Saturday night she went to this big wedding and when she was driving home afterwards, she hit a guy on a bike. She panicked, and just drove off.'

'Oh wow,' breathed Debbie. 'Hit and run! You go to gaol for that.'

Carol nodded. 'Yeah—but according to Lemon, Adair came to her senses later on the same night and went down to the police station and gave herself up. Luckily, it turned out that the guy she hit hadn't been badly hurt at all, and she got off on a good behaviour bond. But Lemon said she's felt guilty about it ever since—and terrified that people in Raven Hill would find out.'

'No wonder,' Debbie said, tossing her head.

'Whether the guy was badly hurt or not, it was still hit and run.'

'At least she went back and confessed in the end,' argued Walter. 'That took nerve.'

Everyone started arguing, then, about whether Ms Adair had been a coward, because she ran away, or incredibly brave, because she went back and confessed. I wriggled out of the group and spotted Liz, waving at me. I went over to her.

'Have you heard?' she asked immediately.

I nodded.

'Isn't it great?' Liz said. 'That Ms Adair decided to tell, I mean. Now she doesn't have a secret any more. And so she's free from Poison Pen. He can do his worst, and he won't hurt her. And she's not leaving Raven Hill! It's wonderful.'

Sunny and Tom came up, both of them grinning. 'Have you heard?' they said together.

They started talking to Liz about how glad they were that we'd made Ms Adair talk to us. They were sure that it was that conversation that had convinced her it was better to face the truth than to run away.

'And she probably realised we really cared about her,' said Liz. 'That would have helped. Even Richelle was nice to her.'

'In a way,' said Sunny dryly. 'I could do without Richelle's advice on dress sense, if I was Ms Adair. Sometimes Richelle is really—'

I tuned out. I was thinking about the other Poison

Pen victims. Ms Adair might have escaped Poison Pen's clutches. But they hadn't. And we'd only discovered a few of them, I was sure of that. For all we knew Raven Hill was filled with desperate people convinced they were about to be in deep trouble. Because of The Eye.

The others might have forgotten about that part of the mystery. But I hadn't. The weekend was coming up. On Monday another Eye column would land on Dad's desk, and he'd have to decide whether to run it or not. I had to get this thing sorted out before then.

After school the gang met up at the gates. 'How about a movie tonight?' Tom suggested. 'I'm temporarily loaded, thanks to Drisk-Haskell and the *Pen* delivery. I feel burdened by cash.'

'You could consider saving your riches for a rainy day,' Liz teased. 'You could consider putting them aside for your university education, or your retirement, maybe.'

Tom put his head on one side and pretended to think about it. Finally he shook his head. 'It's a good thought. A fine thought. But I've decided against it.'

'Listen, speaking of Drisk-Haskell,' drawled Nick, 'are we sacked, or not?'

'I wasn't sure either,' Liz said, grinning. 'So I rang her at lunchtime. And you'll never guess. Apparently, after she'd talked to us, she started to have second thoughts about the way she'd treated Mrs Flower. So she rang the police—and discovered that her ring had been handed in two weeks ago! Somebody had found it on a washbasin in the ladies' room at The Palace. The cops were wondering why no-one had put in a claim for it. Mrs Drisk-Haskell is over the moon.'

'Well, I hope she'll apologise to Mrs Flower,' frowned Sunny.

'She already has!' beamed Liz. 'And she's begged Mrs Flower to come back to her. And Mrs Flower's agreed.'

'Great!' said Richelle, looking very pleased. 'No more house cleaning.'

'No more extra money,' Tom pointed out. 'Ah well—to celebrate our oncoming poverty, how about—'

'Yes, I agree,' said Liz. 'Let's see a movie. But I have to go down to "Craigend" first, to do Pearl Plummer's shopping. Why don't you come with me, and wait in the Glen? I won't be long. Then we can see an early show and have a pizza afterwards.'

'I'll meet you at the Glen,' Richelle said immediately. 'I want to go home and change first.'

Tom looked her up and down. 'What's the matter with the clothes you're wearing?' he enquired. 'They're all right. You don't have to look knock-out gorgeous all the time.'

'Oh, is that so?' she snapped. 'Well, thanks very much!'

She flounced off, leaving Tom to stare after her.

'What did I say?' he asked and Nick raised one eyebrow.

'Don't worry about it, Moysten,' he advised. 'You just put your foot in your mouth, as usual.'

'But how?' Tom insisted. 'I only wanted to know—'

'Forget it, Tom,' Sunny said briskly. 'There's no point trying to understand Richelle. You'll end up as dilly as she is.'

❂

The Glen is a patch of bush between Raven Hill Park and 'Craigend', the old people's home at the end of Craigend Road. We often meet in the Glen. It's a nice place to be—full of birds and the smell of gum leaves.

Liz ran into 'Craigend' to visit Pearl Plummer, and we wandered on to the Glen to wait for her. It was peaceful and beautiful, with the sunlight filtering through the trees and falling in little puddles on the leafy ground.

We sat down in our usual clearing. Nick tried to talk about Poison Pen again, but the rest of us told him to shut up. I lay on my back in the sun, watching the leaves tossing against the background of the blue sky. After all the drama of the last few days, it was great to have the chance to relax and forget about everything. Just as I was starting to doze off, Liz appeared in front of me.

'That was quick,' Sunny commented lazily. 'You

must have done Miss Plummer's shopping at the speed of light.'

'Actually, Pearl's got a cold today,' Liz explained, flopping down beside her. 'She was in bed when I arrived. One of the nurses had got some apples and lemonade for her earlier on, so I just chatted for a while and left. Richelle not here yet?'

'Come on!' jeered Nick, looking at his watch. 'It's only been half-an-hour or something. It takes Richelle that long just to comb her hair.'

But at that moment there was a crackling sound in the undergrowth. Twigs snapped and branches were pushed roughly aside. And then Richelle came storming through the bushes, with leaves in her hair and a smudge of dirt on her cheek. She stopped short, glaring at us.

We all sat up abruptly and stared back at her.

'Hey, Richelle,' said Tom. 'You don't look any different. I mean, you haven't changed.'

'No, I haven't,' she snapped. 'How could I think about what I'm wearing at a time like this?'

'A time like what?' grinned Nick, looking her up and down. 'What could possibly be so serious that you couldn't think about what you looked like?'

'You—you're always teasing me!' shouted Richelle, stamping her foot and looking as if she was about to burst into tears. 'Why don't you *listen*?'

Liz jumped up and went to put her arm around her. 'Richelle, what is it?' she murmured.

'I've had a poison-pen letter!' choked Richelle. 'A really horrible one. And I know who sent it, too.'

14

Contact

Tom lifted his hand to shade his eyes from the sun. 'Hey, I'm impressed,' he chuckled. 'So you've beaten us all to the solution, Richelle. Come on, don't keep us in suspense. Who wrote your poison-pen letter?'

'Don't try to act innocent, Tom,' she said, eyes blazing. 'You did, of course.'

Tom sat bolt upright. He glanced around at the rest of us, looking startled and confused, and then focused on Richelle.

'Are you crazy?' he asked, his voice rising to a sort of squeak. 'Why would I do that?'

'Because—because you're always being mean to me,' gasped Richelle. 'I suppose you thought you'd give me a really good fright, didn't you? You thought, "I'll teach her to be stuck up. She thinks she's so wonderful." Well, I'll—'

'I never did any such thing!' squeaked Tom. 'Show me this letter I'm supposed to have sent. Go on, show me!'

Richelle held out an envelope at arm's length. Tom

tried to grab it but she snatched it away.

'Don't you touch it,' she shouted. 'If I let you get your hands on it, you'll rip it into shreds, so that nobody else can see how mean and spiteful you are.'

Tom went scarlet. You could see that he was really upset.

'Richelle, Tom hasn't written any letter to you,' Sunny said calmly, glancing at him.

'Well, who else would?' Richelle demanded.

'The same person who wrote all the others,' I said quietly. 'Look at the envelope. It's exactly like the ones we've seen before. So unless you think Tom wrote all those too . . .'

'You mean The Eye wrote this? You mean it's a *real* poison-pen letter?'

'Not The Eye,' I reminded her patiently. 'Someone calling themselves The Eye. Can I read this out?'

Richelle shrugged, and brushed back her hair with a shaking hand. I pulled the familiar looking paper out of the envelope and looked at it.

YOU'RE NOT AS SWEET AND INNOCENT AS YOU LOOK, ARE YOU? YOU KNOW IT, THE EYE KNOWS IT, AND SOON EVERYONE ELSE WILL TOO. JUST WAIT.

As usual, the letter was signed 'The Eye'.

We all looked at each other. I could tell that everyone else felt as awful as I did. It had been bad enough when the poison-pen letters were addressed to people we didn't know well. I'd felt sorry for Ms Adair and Mrs Flower and the others, of course, but this was different. It was far worse to see Richelle standing there with a lost, hurt look in her blue eyes.

'See what I mean?' she choked. 'It's awful. I know how Ms Adair felt now. It's terrible to think that someone hates me that much.'

She started to shiver and Liz hugged her protectively. 'You've got an idea, haven't you, Elmo?' she said, glancing over Richelle's shoulder. 'I can tell. Come on, let us in on it, will you?'

'Remember what we said about Poison Pen's victims?' I said slowly. 'Richelle fits the picture perfectly. She's happy and confident—just the sort of person that Poison Pen wants to get at.'

Richelle gave a strangled sob.

'Yes,' Liz said, with a sharp look at me. 'But you know more than that, Elmo.'

'I don't really,' I murmured. 'It's just—an idea I have. But something doesn't fit. I'm trying to work it out. And I didn't really want to talk about it till I know for sure. It wouldn't be fair—to the person concerned.'

'What person concerned?' exploded Nick. He glanced meaningfully at Richelle's tear-stained face. 'Come off it, Zimmer. How bad do things have to get before you'll take a chance?'

'Elmo,' urged Liz. 'Just tell us who you suspect. We won't tell anyone else. And we promise we won't make contact with the person until you give us the word. Okay?'

I stared at her. 'Contact,' I repeated slowly. 'Contact. Of *course*.'

Suddenly I knew what I had to do. 'Come with me,' I said. 'This won't take long. And then I'll tell you everything.'

I jumped to my feet and charged out of the Glen, with the others following close behind. Without saying a word I led them back up Craigend Road to Raven Hill Road and then turned off into the crescent where Mrs Drisk-Haskell lived.

While the rest of the gang waited crossly outside, I hurried up the winding drive, knocked on the door and asked Mrs Drisk-Haskell a single question.

'If it's anything to do with you, yes,' she snapped and shut the door in my face.

I ran back down the drive to the others, with my heart beating like a drum. They could tell by my face that I had the answer.

'Well?' Sunny demanded. 'What did you ask her? And what did she say?'

'I asked her whether she wore contact lenses,' I panted. 'And she said *yes*.'

'What's *that* got to do with anything?' asked Richelle scornfully.

I swallowed hard and looked around at the confused faces around me. I have to admit, I was enjoying being the centre of attention for once. After all, they all had exactly the same information as I had. They should have been able to come to the same conclusions.

'All right, Elmo. Enough's enough. Tell!' Liz commanded.

I grinned at her and got ready to explain. Then, while I was organising the facts in my mind, another piece of the jigsaw suddenly slotted into place. And it was then that I realised that by an incredible stroke of luck I might have solved two mysteries instead of one.

And the second mystery was a whole lot more dangerous than the first.

'I'll tell you,' I said to my friends. 'This is one secret I definitely *don't* want to keep. But there's something else as well. I'm not a hundred per cent sure about it— but I'm sure enough to be scared.'

'Well, we'll help deal with it,' Nick shrugged. 'We've gone through trouble together before, haven't we?'

'If you want to be in on this, you'll have to miss the movie,' I warned.

'Oh who cares about the movie?' Sunny exclaimed. 'Who cares about some stupid movie when we've got the chance of tracking down Poison Pen. Stop dropping all these mysterious hints, Elmo, and tell us what's going on.'

So we talked. Then we went to the *Pen* and talked to Dad. We made some phone calls. And an hour later, the mystery of the poison-pen letters was solved.

After that, we knew there wouldn't be any more nasty letters in Raven Hill, at least from that particular source. But I still had one more thing to do.

At five past six I rang Mr Richardson. 'I still haven't found out who The Eye is,' I said quickly, before he could hang up. 'But I know who's been writing those poison-pen letters, though. Is *that* worth fifty dollars to you?'

I could hear him gasp, and then he cleared his throat. 'Oh, why not?' he said, trying to sound casual. 'It isn't what I asked you about, but you've obviously gone to a lot of trouble. Tell me now and I'll bring the money around on Monday. You have my word on it.'

'Okay then. It's Annette Nudsworth.'

There was silence for a moment. 'Who?' Mr Richardson said doubtfully.

'Annette Nudsworth,' I repeated with a private grin.

'Who is Annette Nudsworth?' he shouted. 'I've never heard that name in my life. I don't know anybody called Annette Nudsworth.'

'Oh yes, you do. So do a lot of people. But we don't know her name. And we don't take any notice of her. I think that's where all the trouble started.'

'Stop playing games and tell me who she is, son,' Mr Richardson begged. 'This is serious.'

He was right. I decided to stop teasing and tell him. 'She's Ms Salamandi's receptionist,' I said. 'You know, the woman who sits behind the desk and files the cards and everything?'

This time the silence lasted even longer. 'Well, I'll be . . .' Mr Richardson said finally. 'Are you sure?'

'Quite sure.'

'Well, well, well,' he sighed. 'I might drop in to see Ms Nudsworth on Monday, then. I think I'd like a few words with her. And with her boss. Thank you very much for the tip.'

He hung up straightaway. I replaced the phone carefully and looked around the room.

'So that's that,' I said.

15

Headlines

Fifteen minutes later a car drew up outside Ms Salamandi's rooms in Craigend Road. Someone got out and went inside.

The waiting room was empty and the only light came from a desk lamp beside the typewriter. The colourless woman at the reception desk didn't even bother to turn around from the filing cabinet where she was putting away the patients' cards.

'We're closed,' she said. 'Ms Salamandi's gone home.'

'That suits me,' the man replied. 'You're the one I need to see, Ms Nudsworth. Regarding some letters that you've been sending.'

The woman's back stiffened. 'I don't know what you mean,' she gasped.

'Oh, I think you do,' the man told her. 'I think you know exactly what I mean.'

She swung around to face him. As he walked

towards her, a gun appeared in his hand.

'I don't know how you found out,' he said conversationally. 'But you should have known better than to mess with me. What were you after? Blackmail, is that it?'

The woman flattened herself against the cabinet. In the small room he could hear her panting with fear.

'I won't tell, Mr Richardson,' she said eagerly. 'I promise I won't say a word.'

His eyes glazed over. 'No, it's too late for that,' he whispered. 'If it had just been a matter of robbery, I might have played along with the blackmail. But a man died, Ms Nudsworth. We're talking about murder here. I can't run the risk of anyone else finding out about that.'

'What—what are you going to do?' she quavered.

Richardson stared down at the gun. 'I can't kill you here,' he said, as if he was thinking out loud. 'That kid at the *Pen* told me about you. He'd be bound to make the connection if you turned up dead straight after that. So I think you'd better just disappear. I'm going to take you for a little drive. Out to the country, maybe. And I'm afraid you won't be coming back.'

The woman cowered away from him in terror. He gestured at her with the gun, smiling to himself.

'When I drop in to see you on Monday, I'll be terribly surprised to find that you've gone. You'll have flown the coop, Ms Nudsworth. Ms Salamandi will be very cross to discover that her nice, easy-to-bully receptionist has let her down so badly. Everyone will think you ran away before you could be unmasked as the poison-pen writer. And now I think it's time—'

He made a sudden grab for the woman. She ducked under his arm and grabbed his wrist, twisting it until the gun dropped from his fingers. As it clattered across the floor, all the lights went on.

Richardson stared around at a room that was suddenly full of police. He bared his teeth as he struggled against the woman's grip.

'Who are you?' he snarled. 'You're not Annette Nudsworth.'

Constable Greta Vortek grinned cheerfully. 'No, I'm not,' she agreed. 'Ms Nudsworth is in a safe place. She's done some stupid things, but she doesn't deserve to die for it. Now, shall we go down to the station, Mr Richardson? You're under arrest.'

○

So that's how the mastermind behind the Raven Hill bank robbery was caught. The cops' plan worked perfectly. They wouldn't let us anywhere near the excitement, of course, but Greta Vortek told Dad and Stephen Spiers—and us—about it afterwards over a cup of coffee in the Black Cat, just as she'd promised.

'Everything worked perfectly,' she said, eyes sparkling. 'Richardson's talking as loud and fast as he can, now. He's dobbing in his crim friends right and left. So all the other staff at the bank can rest easy now. We can't thank you kids enough. The coffee's on me.'

'No, no,' Dad protested immediately. 'The *Pen* got a great story out of this. It's on me.'

While they argued about it, Tom hastily ordered an enormous slice of chocolate cake and Liz leaned over to catch my eye.

'Mum will be so happy this is all over,' she whispered. 'You were brilliant to work out all that stuff about Mr Richardson, Elmo. You really were.'

No-one can whisper quietly enough to escape Nick's sharp ears. 'Yeah—it wasn't bad,' he drawled. 'But it was just a lucky guess, wasn't it?'

I shrugged. 'Not quite. It was just a feeling I had. He was too—too keen. He offered too much money. He tried too hard to be casual. He was too insistent that I shouldn't tell anyone about it. Then he got too angry when we asked him about the poison-pen letters. It all felt wrong.'

'Hang on,' Tom said with his mouth full. He swallowed quickly and added, 'All of Annette Nudsworth's victims were pretty upset, right? I can't see why you thought Richardson was any different.'

'I can,' Liz said straightaway. 'All the others—Sam Frean, Ms Adair, Mrs Drisk-Haskell—basically, they were all dying to confess. They knew they'd done something wrong and they wanted to get it off their chests. They tried to put us off at first, but they caved in pretty quickly. Mr Richardson was the only one who was determined to keep his secret to himself.'

'That's right,' I agreed. 'Once I realised that, I started to wonder whether he had a *really* guilty secret. Something much worse than putting mutton in the lamb mince, or pretending your parents didn't exist—even worse than a hit-and-run accident that happened years ago.'

'Yes, but it could have been *anything*,' Richelle objected. 'He could have had two wives. He could have been embezzling from the bank. He could have been dealing drugs. He—'

'Richelle Brinkley, you've got a criminal mind,' Sunny remarked, staring at her in astonishment.

I grinned at Richelle. 'Actually, I thought about all those things too,' I told her. 'But when I looked at the facts, I realised that there was an obvious secret right under my nose. And why go past that? I thought. Mr Richardson was the manager of the bank. The cops had said that the bank robbers must have had inside help. Well, obviously the manager would have been in the best position to help the thieves. And obviously he'd be terrified if he thought anyone knew about it, especially after the murder.'

Nick nodded thoughtfully. 'Simple,' he commented.

'No, it isn't,' Liz said hotly. 'I still think Elmo was brilliant.'

'Not really,' I said, feeling myself starting to blush. 'I just had a hunch and I followed it through.'

'Spoken like a true newspaper man,' said Stephen Spiers, slapping me on the back. 'Your old grandfather

would have been proud of you.'
After that, I didn't even try to stop the blushing.

16

One last question

'When did you work out about Annette Nudsworth?'
asked Sunny. 'That was a pretty good piece of detective
work as well. When did you realise that she was Poison
Pen?'

'When I saw Richelle's eye exercises.' I paused for a
moment, to enjoy the puzzled looks on their faces, and
then added, 'They were in an envelope that was the
same size and shape as Poison Pen's envelopes, with her
name and address typed in exactly the same way.'

'Rats,' Nick said, looking annoyed. 'I should've
spotted that. But I—'

'You were too busy feeling superior to me, because I
was worried about getting glasses,' Richelle said smugly.
'So was everyone else, except Elmo. Serves you all
right.'

'As soon as I'd picked up on that clue, it all fell
into place,' I went on. 'There was one thing that all of
Poison Pen's victims had in common. They all wore

glasses. Mrs Flower with her cat's-eye glasses. Ms Adair with her tortoiseshell frames. Mr Richardson had those really thick glasses. Sam Frean took out his reading glasses to check his files. Mrs Drisk-Haskell was the only one who didn't fit the pattern. And then I realised. Contact lenses. She could have worn contact lenses.'

'And she did!' sighed Liz.

'Yes, it all fitted together fairly neatly,' I said. 'When Richelle got a letter straight after her visit to the optometrist, I was convinced that Poison Pen was connected with Ms Salamandi's office. After that, it wasn't hard to figure out Poison Pen's identity.'

Tom leaned past me to hijack the slice of cake that Sunny had left half-eaten. 'Ms Salamandi could've been writing the anonymous letters herself, couldn't she?'

Richelle and I looked at each other and burst out laughing.

'You haven't met Ms Salamandi,' I said to Tom. 'She doesn't fit the description of a poison-pen writer at all.'

'That reminds me, why did Annette Nudsworth use The Eye's name to sign her letters?' Liz asked. 'She isn't really The Eye, is she? I mean, she isn't the person who writes the column in the *Pen*.'

'No way,' I said. 'No, I suspect she just chose that name by chance. She was cutting her messages out of newspapers, remember. She must've been using the *Pen* when she spotted The Eye's by-line at the bottom of the column, and decided to use it. It probably appealed to her because she was working for an optometrist—and because she was watching everybody who came into the place.'

Richelle shivered. 'Well, I hope she's learnt her lesson,' she said vengefully.

'I think she has,' Liz assured her. 'Greta was there when the sergeant questioned her. She said she was terrified by what had nearly happened to her—so terrified that she'll never try the same trick again.'

'Yes, she took on more than she could handle,' I agreed. 'She was trying to freak people by making vague, general threats. But of course she had no idea that one of the people she was threatening had actually done something criminal—something so terrible that he'd be willing to kill to hide it.'

There was silence for a moment. Then Tom looked around at us with a broad grin.

'Well done, team,' he said. 'I think I might have one last piece of cake, just to celebrate.'

None of Annette Nudsworth's victims pressed charges in the end. I guess they were all too embarrassed to go into court. Imagine standing up in front of a whole room full of people and repeating your deepest secrets out aloud.

Annette resigned from her job and moved away

from Raven Hill. Even if Ms Salamandi had let her stay, which is unlikely, her life wouldn't have been worth living in that office. She would have been forced to face her ex-victims every time they came in to have their eyes tested. And they wouldn't have been too happy to see her, to put it mildly.

The *Pen* published a brief account of the anonymous letters. There was no mention of Annette Nudsworth's name, of course—just enough information to let any other victims know that they were safe now. Dad didn't even have to write the story. It turned up in The Eye's column when it arrived in the office the Monday after all the excitement.

'Fascinating,' Dad murmured as he read through the copy. 'The Eye really does see everything that goes on in Raven Hill.'

'That's one mystery you didn't solve, mastermind,' said Nick, looking over Dad's shoulder. 'We still don't know the first thing about The Eye.'

I shrugged. 'At least we know The Eye doesn't write poison-pen letters.'

'You *never* thought it,' Liz said. 'You always said The Eye wouldn't do a thing like that. You've got good instincts about that kind of stuff, Elmo.'

She smiled at me and I smiled back, feeling rather guilty. I shouldn't really have been taking the credit for having good instincts. After all, who would know better than me that The Eye was innocent?

Seeing that I'm The Eye myself.

Mind you, as Sunny once said, 'Even Elmo's probably got something to hide.'

And I think this is one secret that I intend to keep. The mystery of The Eye is never going to be solved.

Even by Teen Power Inc.

THE BAD DOG MYSTERY

Emily Rodda

There's *no way* Richelle is joining the rest of the gang looking after Jock – the worst-behaved dog in the world. She has enough problems of her own. But when Jock faces real trouble, Richelle is there to help him. And who knows – maybe Jock will return the favour sometime . . .

BREAKING POINT

Emily Rodda

The gang are thrilled that they're helping well-known mystery-writer, Abner Cain, finish his latest book. But there's a sinister mystery surrounding Mr Cain, and Liz is determined to solve it.

Before she reaches Breaking Point . . .

The Raven Hill Mysteries

THE SECRET OF BANYAN BAY

Emily Rodda

Tom and his friends are trying to relax in the peaceful coastal town of Banyan – but things aren't quite going to plan. Weird things are happening, and Tom wants to find out more. Soon he's out of his depth, struggling in the hands of a ruthless, unknown enemy – one who holds the secret of Banyan Bay . . .

Raven Hill Mysteries
Emily Rodda

All Hodder Children's books are available at your local bookshop or newsagent, or can be ordered direct from the publisher. Just tick the titles you want and fill in the form below. Prices and availability subject to change without notice.

Hodder Children's Books, Cash Sales Department, Bookpoint, 39 Milton Park, Abingdon, OXON, OX14 4TD, UK. If you have a credit card you may order by telephone – (01235) 831700.

Please enclose a cheque or postal order made payable to Bookpoint Ltd to the value of the cover price and allow the following for postage and packing:
UK & BFPO – £1.00 for the first book, 50p for the second book, and 30p for each additional book ordered up to a maximum charge of £3.00.
OVERSEAS & EIRE – £2.00 for the first book, £1.00 for the second book, and 50p for each additional book.

Name...

Address...

....

....

If you would prefer to pay by credit card, please complete:
Please debit my Visa/Access/Diner's Card/American Express (delete as applicable) card no:

Signature..

ExpiryDate...